AFTONHOUSE

By Jan-Andrew Henderson

Black Anvil – Blue Rose Press
An Imprint of
Three Ravens Publishing
Chickamauga, GA USA

Table of Contents

History repeats itself only in that, from afar, we all seem to lead exactly the same life. We are all born; we all spend time here on earth; we all die. But up close, we have each walked down our own separate paths. We have stood at our own lonely crossroads. We have touched the lives of others at crucial points, for better or for worse. In the end, each of us has lived a unique life story, astounding and complicated, a story that could never be repeated.
Edward Bloor
Things are sweeter when they're lost. I know-because once I wanted something and got it. It was the only thing I ever wanted badly, Dot, and when I got it, it turned to dust in my hand.
F. Scott Fitzgerald. *The Beautiful and Damned*

For those who knew Spiral Wood

Prologue

Dark and Her Child

Dark Arrowsmith tucked her son into bed.

"Can I have a story?" the boy asked.

"Getting pretty late," Dark warned. "It'll have to be short."

"What about *Jimmy Jones and the Giant Buttock from Space*?"

"That's got more pages than *War and Peace*."

"Let's do *War and Peace* then." The child looked hopeful. "Does it have any bums?"

"Probably. I've never read it." Dark thought for a moment. "How about I tell you a fairy tale instead?"

"I'm not a kid, mum."

"You're four."

"Oh. All right, then."

Dark got comfortable and began to talk.

Once upon a time, there was a powerful Laird who lived in a great house on a hill overlooking the village of Aftonhouse. A Laird is like a Lord, only with more tartan.

The Laird had an only son who he heartily disapproved of. You see, the youth had fallen in love with a young girl. Not a lady or princess, just an ordinary country lass. Certainly, she was very beautiful but she didn't have any money or titles. Even worse, she was a foreigner with a funny accent. It simply wasn't the done thing.

But the young man was determined to marry her and nobody could talk him out of it. The Laird thought of locking this potential bride away in a dungeon. But then, he'd have to feed her and make all sorts of excuses as to where she'd gone, so he finally relented.

Soon, a date for the wedding was set. The Laird reluctantly declared a public holiday and the village was decorated with bunting for the big event.

The day before the marriage was to occur, the young man organised festivities in the forest on Clachan Hill. But, as everyone knows, it's unlucky for a bride and groom to see each other before the wedding, so they promised faithfully to stay on either side of the woods.

The lass and the other village maidens took the north side. There, they picnicked, made garlands of flowers and drank pear juice. The young man and his well-to-do friends played hide and seek on the south slope. These were simpler times, you see.

While his friends counted, the young man made his way deep up into the forest until he wasn't sure where he was. There, he came across a hollow tree.

"Perfect," he cried. "They'll never suss me out here."

The opening was very small. However, by wriggling his shoulders, he managed to worm his way right inside. Unfortunately, he found himself stuck, with nobody to hear his muffled cries.

His friends searched and searched but, by the time they found the young man, he had suffocated.

"This is a pretty creepy story," the child objected.

"His bum was sticking out of the tree," Dark said. "If that helps."

"Yeah. Much better."

Now the friends were in a real pickle. The Laird was powerful and would not take kindly to his only child dying in their care. Crying and berating themselves, they quickly buried the young man and hid his grave.

After that, they concocted a lie to cover their butts.

"More butts," the child said. "I'm starting to like this story."

Dark smiled and carried on.

They told the Laird his son had gotten cold feet about the wedding and decided to go off and seek his fortune in the city. The fact that he was already heir to his dad's wealth, so had absolutely no need for extra funds, didn't seem to occur to anyone. Which just goes to show having a lot of money and power doesn't make you more intelligent than anyone else.

The Laird was actually quite pleased by this turn of events. It meant his son wouldn't be marrying a commoner and might come back with some cash of his own.

The lass, however, did not believe the lies of these so-called friends. She and the young man were madly in love and she knew he would never have abandoned her without good reason.

Everyone else went on with their lives but she wouldn't give up. Each day, she searched the forest in vain for her vanished beau.

One evening, as the light was fading, she came across an ancient enchantress picking secret herbs for her spells. The lass begged for help and the old woman got so fed up with the girl following her around crying she eventually yielded.

She offered the maiden a trade. The enchantress would bring back this lost love if the girl gave her something precious in return. The lass said she had nothing to offer but youth and beauty.

"That'll do nicely," the crone replied. "I haven't looked my best these last hundred or so years."

She used magic to locate the young man's grave but his body had turned to dust by then. Still, a bargain is a bargain, so she did her best.

She turned the girl into a white doe and the young man into a black hart. That's male deer if you're not up to speed on hoofed ruminant mammals. After that, she went off into town to find the nearest mirror and get her hair done.

But the old woman did not know the young man and his fiancée had faithfully promised to stay on either side of the hill until they were wed. And enchanted creatures cannot break a promise.

Therefore, they were destined to always remain apart, lamenting that both were so close to each other yet so far away.

When the Laird realised he would never see his son again, he grew remorseful, locked himself away in an ivory tower and died of a broken heart. After that, Aftonhouse became a beacon for the vanished, lonely and accursed. A sad and beautiful place where they could forget and be forgotten.

The end.

"What a weird story," the child said. "Did you make it up?"

"Sort of." Dark smiled at him. "I'm a writer, after all. That's what I do."

"It was pretty good, I suppose," he relented. "Is it true?"

"It's a parable. Based on events that took place before you were born."

"OK. Can I have *Jimmy and the Giant Buttock from Space* tomorrow? Or maybe some iPad time?"

"You can." The woman stroked his hair. "It'll be Friday and no school next day, so you can have as much iPad as you like."

"Awesome!" the boy beamed. "I won't be able to sleep for dreaming about it."

"Excuse me?" Dark blinked rapidly. "*What* did you just say?"

"I love the weekend." Her son rolled over and pulled the covers to his chin. "You too, mum."

"Love you more. Goodnight." Dark kissed his head and tiptoed from the room, her heart pounding.

She crept downstairs, poured a whisky and took it into her study. Then she sat and stared at the computer.

"You look like you're about to start writing," her partner said from the doorway. "What's the latest masterpiece going to be about?"

"You and I," she said. "And all the things that happened in this place. It's time."

"A comedy then." He grinned awkwardly. "Or is it a tragedy?"

"Bit of both, I guess." She smiled at him over her shoulder.

"But, mostly, it's a love story."

-Part I-

Into the paradise our younger lives made of this bed and room
Has leaked the world and all its questioning
and now those shapes terrify us most
that remind us of our own. Easier now
to check longings and sentiment,
to pretend not to care overmuch,
you look out across the years, and you come to me
quiet as the last of our senses closing.
Brian Patten. *you come to me quiet as rain not yet fallen*

The Road to Aftonhouse 2024

Dark Arrowsmith

Dark sang as she drove.

After she'd used up her repertoire, she hesitated. Normally, she would have belted out half-familiar songs, making up the words as she went along. These days, she wasn't in the right frame of mind to be fooled by her own false levity.

Boredom overcame her, so she put on the radio and had another go, trying to outperform some bimbette's vocal gymnastics.

I'm fed up. The world is shit. My life is dull. I'm tired of it.

I used to be a rebel and I loved to drink and fuck.

Now I'm in the Scottish highlands, where I bet I'm out of luck.

She gave up again, though her lyrics were better than the real ones. Something about how the singer was empowered enough to wear green lipstick but obviously not empowered enough to use her natural voice.

Dark was in a foul mood.

Mountains rose on all sides like jagged, mouldy molars. The sky turned a deep bluish-black, streaked with orange, as if the vista around her had been punched in the mouth. Reception faded, so she turned off the radio. Glanced at a small box in the passenger seat, containing mementos from the love of her life. When she reached her destination, she intended to find out what had happened to him or bury them forever.

Perhaps both.

She stopped for coffee and brought it back to the car. A sign across the road said **Aftonhouse. 20 Miles.** On impulse, she opened the box and rifled through it until she found a homemade birthday card. On the front was a beautifully rendered drawing of her. Inside was an inscription.

To Dark.
All my love. Always. Always.
Spiral.

Jolly Judge. Edinburgh 2023
Dark, Spiral and Lewis

Spiral Wood. Oddly handsome, strangely disarming, older than Dark and always dressed in black. God knows how he got the name because he gave everyone a different explanation. Even her.

She met him in the Jolly Judge bar in Edinburgh.

Dark had wandered in, lacking anything else to do, lonely and drawn to the bright lights and noise. The small pub was busy but Spiral and his friend, Lewis, were at one end of a long wooden table - and the other side was unoccupied. Dark sat down and pretended to ignore them, staring into space and trying to look like she belonged.

Spiral was reading out loud from a bit of paper and sounded drunk.

"Life... is a tiny transition between the eternity before we're born and the eternity after we die," he announced. "An eye blink in a nothingness that will last forever."

"S'cuse me?" she said, before realising he was talking to Lewis. To Dark's consternation, they took it as a sign she wanted to be part of their conversation.

"Once or twice in our lives," Spiral continued, turning to her. "We linger on the reality of what death entails for a second too long. Then we feel the horror of realisation, in a brief crystal-sharp agony of sickening fear...."

He opened the bit of paper.

"...Happy birthday."

"Brings a tear to my eye," Lewis said. "Not for the reasons you think, though."

"Imagine giving anyone a birthday card like that?" Spiral asked her. "No? That's why I couldn't sell it to Hallmark."

Dark wasn't sure if he wanted her to comment, yet it was an opening she couldn't resist.

"Happens to be *my* birthday," she remarked.

"Then you can't sit on your own," Spiral gasped. "Come and join us."

He spotted her doubtful look.

"Honestly, we aren't looking to pick anyone up. We don't talk about sport and we're not serial killers."

"That'll certainly put her at ease," Lewis grunted. "You had to mention sport."

"I quite like cricket," Dark ventured.

"Nobody's perfect." Spiral grinned. "My grandfather once ate a telephone box."

"Feel free to ignore us if you're waiting for someone," Lewis added tactfully. "We're rather unsavoury characters and, as you probably already noticed, Spiral is a compulsive liar."

"Only when I'm talking."

She looked at them both and made a snap decision. What the fuck? She'd come to Scotland for adventure, after all. Most backpackers were in their teens. She hadn't plucked up the courage to travel until she was in her thirties.

"Not waiting for anyone." She slid along the bench towards them. "I'm from Australia and only arrived in Scotland yesterday. Always wanted to see it."

"Excellent choice of destination." Spiral shook her hand. "I'm Spiral Wood. Failed entrepreneur and rotten salesman. Spiral's just a nickname, of course. Lewis came up with it. It's a lot nicer than most of the things he calls me."

"I'm Dorothy Arrowsmith but people usually just use Dot."

Spiral squinted at her dark curly bob, black polo neck and jeans, an outfit that almost mirrored his own. He seemed to be trying to focus properly.

"Can I call you Dark instead?"

"Why?" The woman was taken aback. "What's wrong with Dot?"

"It's too insignificant. You deserve something more… exotic."

"Dark Arrowsmith does sound pretty cool," Lewis agreed. "A superhero name, even."

He glanced from one to the other and sniggered.

"You look like a pair of matching book ends."

"I suppose that's OK, then," Dark conceded.

"This is Lewis," Spiral indicated his friend. "I don't know what kind of ideas he has. I've never asked."

"Pleased to meet you, doll," Lewis nodded. "You've now heard all about me."

She took to them immediately. Lewis was tall and muscular, with a classically square jaw and a wit so dry it could soak up the sea. Spiral was full of nonsense and false bravado, doing his best to hide something intrinsically empty and sad. Dark didn't understand how she knew that so quickly. She just did. His verbal diarrhoea should have been annoying but was always delivered with self-deprecating charm.

She threw caution to the wind and jumped on their train of thought.

"So… Spiral? You're a compulsive liar."

"Don't believe anything Lewis says." The man threw up his hands in mock horror. "I'm just a common or garden liar. White ones. Little ones."

"How can you tell the size of a lie?" Dark asked coolly. "You got a measuring tape?"

"I did. But Lewis borrowed it to make a dress." Spiral nudged his friend. "Anyway, it's the truth that hurts. And love, of course."

"That's what the best songs say," the big man agreed. "They also say breaking up is hard to do... and, yes we have no bananas."

"Say, for instance, I bump into Lewis's mum," Spiral winked at her. "And she wants another one-night stand."

Lewis gave a loud sigh.

"I'm not going to tell her I was drunk and mistook her for the yoga instructor down the hall. I tell her, can't get her out of my head and I've definitely got five minutes to spare."

"I doubt she's that desperate," Dark snorted.

"You never met my mum." Lewis rolled his eyes. "Neither did Spiral, or he wouldn't be going there."

"Lies are building blocks for a nicer world, Dark," Spiral chuckled. "Truth is for people who don't have the imagination to think up a good story."

"Rotten salesman? Spiral could sell you the Great Wall of China." Lewis hiccupped and finished his pint. "That's the only man-made structure you can see from space, by the way. Except you can't tell what it is."

"That's what makes it so easy to sell."

"You two have been in this pub for quite some time, huh?" Dark chuckled.

"In Edinburgh, there's a famous mansion." Spiral was obviously on a roll. "John Knox's house? Big tourist attraction. You might have ha..."

"I read about John Knox," Dark interrupted. "I read all about Edinburgh."

"Did you know he never lived there? It was a lie concocted to stop the building being demolished."

"The guidebook didn't mention that."

"Dutch Pennsylvania? The original settlers were German." Spiral slurred his words slightly, trying to pronounce Pennsylvania. "Richard III wasn't a hunchback and he didn't kill the princes in the tower. You can't actually see the Great Wall of China from space. The Spanish inquisition mainly took place in France and John Wayne never fought in a war."

"The Spanish inquisition?" Dark laughed. "How did we suddenly get there?"

"Ha!" Lewis pursed his lips. "Nobody expects the Spanish inquisition."

"I'll stop complaining." Spiral cheered up momentarily. "I just get tired of people twatting on about what's true and ignoring what's necessary."

"Like what?"

"Like tackling climate change or pollution." He pulled a face. "I'm scared to eat tinned tuna in case my tongue drops off."

"It's not tuna that's going to make your tongue drop off," Lewis smirked. "And you're still complaining."

"I'm complaining that all we do is shuffling problems around, like kids raking up leaves," Spiral finished. "Putting them in a heap and pretending that's a solution."

"Spiral likes to run through piles of leaves and scatter them in the air," Lewis said. "Fun to do, but people just frown and rake them up again."

"It's called leaving." Spiral finished his pint. "And I'm going to have to. As you can probably tell, Dark, I drank rather more than I intended."

"Me too, but I'm off to the toilet first." Lewis got up and weaved unsteadily out of the room. Spiral took a huge breath and visibly pulled himself together.

"I'm sorry. I've been spouting all kinds of rubbish and not giving you a chance to talk." He seemed genuinely abashed. "I'm pissed and I apologise."

The slur had vanished from his voice, so he suddenly seemed sober.

"Would you like to meet us here tomorrow when I'm not being an asshole? I can buy you a proper birthday drink… eh… Dot."

"Dark is fine," the girl smiled. "I kind of like it."

"Will I take that as a yes?"

"If you promise to throw in a little sport."

"Not cricket, though." Spiral shook his head violently. "I absolutely won't talk about that. The Scottish national cricket team would probably lose to the average Australian primary school netball squad. Not that I know anything about either."

"Fair enough." Her smile widened. "Goodnight, Spiral."

"Night, toots. I'll collect Lewis on the way out. Guy's got a terrible sense of direction and is probably back at the bar."

He leaned towards her.

"He got dumped today, so I was trying to cheer him up. Only, I don't know how."

He patted her arm and left.

After they were gone, Dark hugged herself happily. Within a day of arriving, she had a new name and new friends.

What's more, both of them were rather cute.

Dark's Cottage 2024

Dark Arrowsmith

Dark arrived in Aftonhouse Glen after nightfall. She had rented a small holiday cottage and the key was under the mat. It was pitch black but she could hear the sound of running water somewhere close. She let herself in then quickly explored the place. The main room was snug, with oak beams, a small TV and puffy floral sofas. The bedroom had a huge king-sized bed and a leather armchair piled high with towels. There was an oak dining table in the kitchen and a genuine Agar under hanging brass pots.

"Not too shabby."

Dark put on the kettle to make tea, then opened the fridge. Inside, she found a bottle of wine with a welcome note from the landlady, so she opened them instead. She fetched Spiral's box of mementos from her car and dumped it on the living room floor.

"This is your life distilled into two feet by two feet," she muttered. "A little shrine dedicated to someone I loved but never really knew."

She was pretty sure Spiral would agree with that summation.

"That's not good enough for me."

She sank onto the couch, holding a full glass and stared at the box.

Spiral Wood.

He took his ideas to the pub and made them dance, like Charlie Chaplin with little French rolls on brass forks, a clown conjuring magic out of stale bread.

Spiral could twist a situation until even he couldn't recognise it, Dark thought. Perhaps that's how he got the name. He lived in such a storm of leaves it was hard to see him properly.

Now she was raking through the debris for clues. The truth was in Aftonhouse somewhere and she was determined to find it.

She heaved a sigh and let the memories flood back.

Jolly Judge. Edinburgh 2023

Dark, Spiral and Lewis

The next night, Dark went to the same pub. This time she had put on makeup, a short black velvet dress and thigh-high leather boots. Spiral and Lewis were at the same table and she plonked herself next to them.

"Hi Dark." Spiral waggled his fingers sheepishly at her. "You look nice."

"Welcome, doll. I'll get you a drink." Lewis stood. "What are you having?"

"Whisky and pineapple, please."

"Eh?" he paled. "The barman will remove my knacks with the pickled egg spoon if I ask for that."

"You don't really need them at the moment," Spiral's chuckle turned quickly into a grimace. "Too soon, buddy?"

"You *think*?"

"I was kidding," Dark said placatingly. "I'll have a pint of Belhaven, whatever that is."

Lewis breathed a sigh of relief and went to order.

"So?" She turned to Spiral. "What's up?"

"Well, we're a lot soberer than last night," He gave a beguiling smile. "This time, Lewis and I are having a normal conversation."

"About what?"

"Newtonian mechanics. But we can go back to weird stuff if you want."

"My uncle Gerry once climbed a telegraph pole to rescue a stranded koala and it tore his ear off. That weird enough for you?"

Spiral stroked his stubbled chin, trying to decide if her statement was true or not. Dark counted that as a win.

"I was talking about shagging," Lewis returned. "Which is a polite Scottish word for lovemaking. Something I am not doing anymore. Ever."

"Lewis is still bitter about his latest breakup," Spiral explained.

"That's putting it mildly." The big man sat down. "Your uncle Gerry ever shag a telegraph pole?"

"Only a couple of Polish Poles." Dark accepted the drink. "Ever shag a Newtonian mechanic?"

"Not that I recall. But Spiral probably has, being quite the ladies' man." Lewis sipped his pint. "I'm surprised he hasn't got some girlie in tow tonight."

"If you're coming to a cattle market, you don't bring your own livestock," Spiral replied solemnly. Then he burst out laughing.

"Sorry, couldn't resist that."

"No offence taken." Dark clinked his glass. "I'm getting used to you two."

"Lewis and I subscribe to the Swedish model of intercourse," Spiral explained. "The Swedes consider small talk as dödprat, or dead talk. We prefer rambling drivel."

"Hah!" Lewis guffawed. "That's not how Spiral usually uses the words Swedish model and intercourse in a sentence."

As the night wore on, the conversation flowed smoothly and Dark felt totally at ease with her companions, even though they were virtual strangers.

"I'm having a pretty good time," Spiral announced. "What about you, toots?"

"I must be, considering how many pints I've consumed. Lewis?"

"I think I've died and gone to Helensburgh," the big man burped. "I've forgotten all about Alison."

Dark glanced at Spiral.

"Alison wasn't good enough for you," he consoled. "She should have gone out with me instead."

"Not helping, bud," Lewis scowled. "Besides, she had taste. Thought *you* were a dick."

"A huge dick?"

"Enormous."

"Fair enough." Spiral levelled a finger at Dark. "All right. I got questions."

"What you got?"

"Loads. We don't know anything about you."

"Age before beauty, mate."

"Ha! What goes around comes around," Lewis said smugly. "That's from *The Hand That Rocks the Cradle*, though I can't recall ever seeing the hand."

"Lewis is rather unobservant," Spiral scoffed. "Even missed the Great Wall of China."

"Why are you really called Spiral?" Dark asked.

"I'm kinda fascinated by neurology and how the mind works," he replied. "Big on determinism. Y'know? Eventually, Lewis started calling me Spiral."

He swirled one finger in the air.

"After the double helix DNA thingy?"

"Lewis told me it was because you'd screwed so many girls."

"I was making conversation while you were at the bar," the big man said innocently.

"As I said, ruled by what's in our jeans." Spiral breezed over the comment. "To be honest, girls are a mystery to me. So, I'm trying to find out as much as I can before settling down. Starting with anatomy."

"You are headed for eternal damnation, bud."

"Then I best go to the loo first." Spiral got up and threaded his way through the throng. "Look at the bloody line."

It was the first time Dark had spent more than a few minutes alone with Lewis all night. She finally plucked up the courage to ask.

"This might sound dumb, but do you think he likes me? I can't tell. He doesn't often look people in the eye."

"Yeah. It's a Swedish thing."

"You didn't answer my question."

"You've got a pretty face, tits and the ability to move from one bar to another." The answer was delivered with a smile but still much blunter than she expected. "Of course he does."

"That's a bit harsh. You getting protective of me? Or him?"

"Spiral's my best mate and I care about him." Lewis swirled a finger through the air in an unconscious imitation of his friend's earlier movement. "But he's good at twisting his way into people, then backing out and leaving a hole. *That's* how he got his name."

"I'm not offering to have his babies, Lew. I meant, does he like me as a person?"

"That's what we all say about prospective partners. We look for a handsome prince to be our soulmate, dissect him and find a frog underneath. Then, instead of giving up, we start digging for a soul."

"Very poetic. What's that from?"

"Believe it or not, I made it up myself," the man sniffed. "But, yes, he likes you a lot."

As Spiral came back, Lewis downed his pint and rose.

"I've had a fine time but I'm heading home. Night all."

"So soon?" Spiral looked perplexed. "It's early."

"I can't stare into the abyss with you pair breathing down my neck. Besides, I got shit to do." He kissed Dark on top of her head. "You're quite something, by the way. Good job I've sworn off romance, or you'd be getting both barrels of the famous Lew charm."

Then he was gone.

"He takes breakups pretty hard." Spiral stared after Lewis. "Yet he brings it on himself. He's got no problem attracting girls then doesn't seem interested enough to keep them."

"That's more or less what he said about you."

"Really? No wonder we get on so well."

"I feel sorry for him," Dark said. "He's a lovely guy."

"He's certainly taken with you." Spiral looked down at her. "So am I, to be honest."

He shrugged nonchalantly.

"Time for me to get a drink, now I've embarrassed myself yet again."

Dark watched as he went and ordered another round. Had he just tried to pick her up? She wasn't sure. She wasn't sure of anything about him.

"Happy birthday." Spiral came back and handed her a glass of champagne.

"Thank you!" Dark was touched.

"Don't get much call for fancy tipples in this pub. Barman had to run out to the supermarket next door for a bottle of fizz."

"So." She waited until he sat opposite her. "You going to tell me about yourself, Mr. Wood?"

"Not much to tell, I'm afraid."

"Sum it up in one paragraph, then."

"You could say I'm an observer," Spiral chuckled. "I'm not adding to this world. I'm not subtracting from it. I'm not supporting it, condemning it, changing it, rejoicing in it, getting mad at it or hiding from it. I'm just living in it."

"But it does sound like you'll write a country and western song about it."

"There is, indeed, a possibility that I will write a country and western song about it." He sat back. "Your turn. One paragraph."

"I'll do better than that. One sentence."

"All right."

"I want everything."

Spiral stared at her for a long time.

"I'll be honest," he said, finally. "I find you extremely attractive but, more importantly, I very much enjoy your company."

He hesitated, then plunged on.

"Listen. It's loud and sweaty in here and I have wine and decent music at my house. I don't want to be too forward but… you wanna come with me? Just to talk."

He put a hand to his heart.

"I'm not trying anything on and I'll call you a taxi home whenever you say."

Dark held his gaze. She'd come to Scotland for adventure, after all.

"You had me at wine," she replied. "I don't really like champagne."

Spiral's Flat. Edinburgh 2023

Dark and Spiral

Dark sat on the couch and took off her coat and boots while Spiral Wood fetched wine and poured two glasses.

"What would you like to listen to?" he asked. "Rolf Harris?"

"Very droll," Dark accepted the drink. "I don't mind. What kind of stuff are you into?"

"I'm fond of yodeling, 1970s punk, dub reggae, Norwegian thrash, early Calypso, minimalism and electro-pop." He looked uncomfortable. "I don't much keep up with trends."

"Eclectic." Dark sipped her wine. "I should have known."

"I'll put it on shuffle." Spiral came back and sat at her feet. "I prefer the floor if you don't mind."

"Not at all. Any excuse to look down on you." They clinked glasses. "So. Where so we begin?"

"With what?"

"Getting to know each other," she grinned. "Let me say first, I'm not usually so trusting with men."

"That's cause we're shit," Spiral shot back. "I'll do my best, though. No feelings will be hurt in the making of this conversation."

Dark looked around the room. There were antique cameras, art supplies and an old typewriter perched on various shelves. A computer desk with an expensive laptop. A guitar and, strangely, several battered old violins piled in one corner.

"Do you play?"

"I can manage *Jingle Bells* and *the Violin concerto in D minor* by Sibelius," Spiral shrugged. "Not at the same time, though."

On the walls were a few old film posters in frames, most with titles Dark had never heard of. There was also a painting of a slim and stunning woman in bright blue and yellow. It looked original.

Spiral spotted her quizzical glance.

"Ex-girlfriend," he said, neglecting to give her name.

"That must put off a few prospective dates."

"She deserves to be there," Spiral replied. "Put up with enough crap from me in the short time we were together."

"It's very good." The picture had captured an aloof melancholy, Dark thought. She wondered if the person was really like that. "Did you paint it?"

"Yeah," he stated simply. She liked how he showed no sort of pride at being so accomplished or invited any further comments on his obvious talent.

"Wow."

"So, why are you here?" Spiral asked. "In Scotland, I mean."

Dark thought for a second. But she wasn't ready to tell the whole truth.

"Small town girl who ditched her fiancée and went looking for excitement because she doesn't know exactly what she wants from life or how to get it if she did."

"You're very good at summing yourself up in one sentence," Spiral laughed. "Fortunately, I've never been one for asking too many questions. You find out more about people by chatting to them."

"Chatting?" Dark burst out laughing. "How old are you? Seventy?"

"Torment me not," Spiral scowled. "Or I'll show off my collection of knitting patterns. Anyway, you must be a good ten years younger than me."

"And I care not." Dark slipped onto the floor beside him and filled her glass again. "I feel very much at ease."

"We get on well," Spiral agreed.

"What do you sell, Spiral Wood? Luxury goods?" Dark looked around. "This is a pretty decent apartment."

"It is," he agreed. "There's even a tennis court next door, with floodlights and everything. At night, it looks like a thirties German expressionist movie set."

"Do you play?" she repeated.

"I've tried, but I leap around like Douglas Fairbanks junior in shorts. Floodlight that and it has a truly unnerving effect on both the opposition and my self-esteem."

"I noticed you avoided the question of what you sell."

"A lot of different things." He put his head in both hands and stared at the ground. "Ach, I may as well be truthful, then call you a cab."

"That bad, huh? Insurance? Timeshares in Portugal?" She snapped her fingers. "Gold-plated taps?"

"All of the above, if necessary."

"I don't understand."

"At the moment, Lewis and I are con men." He held up a hand. "But not bad ones."

"Isn't a good con man even worse?" Dark didn't know how to react to that. "What do you do? Cheat old ladies out of their life savings?"

"Of course not!" His shock was genuine. "We only target dodgy businesses who can afford the losses. We are *very* careful not to hurt anybody."

"Why tell me about it at all? Knowing it would put me off you."

"Because I don't want to lie. I like you too much." He picked at his lip. "Shall I phone that taxi?"

"No," Dark said. "I'm not ready to go and I don't have much cash to inveigle."

"Inveigle?"

"Believe it or not, some Aussies own a dictionary."

"Tell me about where you come from," Spiral perked up. "There's a good start."

"I was born in a place called Yorkey's Knob…"

"I'm serious," he interrupted. "I want to know."

"It's in Queensland, dummy. Their local slogan is *Yorkey's Knob, bigger than Moby's Dick.*"

"Holy mother of Christ."

"Small town with small ideas and nothing to do but fuck and watch gardening shows. I left when I finally got sick of having my legs wider than my horizons."

"You come up with that?" Spiral laughed.

"Saw it on a gardening show." Dark scratched her lip. "Mum was the same, I guess. When I was a teen, she quit a lucrative career as a communications officer and opened a little studio, painting woodland scenes on saw blades."

"Brave move." Spiral sounded impressed.

"Unfortunately, my dad left us for another communications officer."

"Oh."

"No biggie. I'm over it."

"Is there a market for saw blades in Australia?"

"There is, actually. Just not painted ones." Dark took a swig of her wine. "Sorry, I don't mean to complain."

"It's all right. I've stopped listening." Spiral poured himself another glass. "Wanna know my trick with parents?"

"Sterilization?"

"Distance. Step back far enough and they are..." he held up a finger and thumb, as an artist would, framing the room. "Another pair of wee threads woven into the fabric of a society you're not interested in wearing."

"Spoken like a true misanthrope. You don't like people much, do you?"

"I don't even like plants." Spiral grinned and nudged her. She didn't move away and their shoulders remained touching.

"You warning me off, mate?" Dark could feel the heat from his body but, strangely enough, he had no smell - as if he were a ghost. "You seem to be."

"I got brands of fruitcake named after me." Spiral sighed. "Been called selfish, irresponsible, cavalier, immature and emotionally vapid. And that's just by Lewis."

"You missed out filled with self-loathing."

"More of a quirk." He stopped suddenly. "Hey. We're supposed to be talking about you."

"You'll want a cigarette first. To fortify yourself for the ordeal."

"How did you know that?" Spiral looked surprised.

"You keep glancing at the packet on your bookcase," Dark smirked. "I wouldn't mind one too."

"Lewis is right. You really are something," Spiral turned to her. "I have to say, I'm a bit smitten."

"You're not so bad yourself." Dark took a deep breath, then leaned forwards and kissed him.

She sensed he had been waiting for the moment. He pulled her close and she slid into his arms. When their lips finally parted, Dark gave a small exhalation.

"Damn. You're good at that." She held up a hand. "I ought to warn you, I don't do one-night stands with people I like."

"What about people you don't like?"

"Yeah. That's not such a problem."

"Suppose I asked you back here again? I'm going to anyway, no matter what happens."

Dark looked into his eyes. Decided this man was part of the escapade she craved.

"Then I'll stay. Still want that cigarette?"

"Later." Spiral put a hand behind her head and kissed her again.

He wasn't clumsy, unsure or hesitant, so Dark abandoned any pretence at nervousness. They removed each other's clothes, still sitting on the floor and, finally, he led her to the bedroom. There, they pressed against each other, gasping and moaning until they came at the same moment.

"Fuck me sideways, that was fun." Dark rolled onto her stomach.

"I might have already done that." Spiral kissed her freckled shoulder. "I thought my heart was going to burst, just then."

"So… you don't want a cigarette and more wine?"

"Only if you stay naked."

"Pretty late to be getting all shy with you now, huh?" Dark took his hand. "Let's go."

And they sat, laughing and talking, without a stitch of clothing, long into the night.

Dark's Cottage 2024

Dark and Lewis

Dark finished her bottle of wine and got into bed. In her hand was a faded photograph she had retrieved from Spiral's memento box. Fortified with alcohol, she got out her mobile and dialed. A sleepy voice answered at the other end.

"It's me, Lew," she said. "Dark Arrowsmith."

How are you, doll? It's been a wee while.

"I'm fine. I'm in a place called Aftonhouse Glen. Staying in a little cottage here."

There was silence for a long time.

You're looking for answers about Spiral, Lewis said eventually. *That's why you're calling.*

"Completely right. I'm a sucker."

I haven't got any, he replied morosely. *Why do you think there are clues at this Aftonhouse place? I've never heard of it.*

"An old polaroid I found hidden in a book. It's a picture of a young boy and I'm pretty sure it's him."

And?

"He's standing in a village street. There's a shop behind him that says *Fr. Cameron: Licenced Grocery store* and next to it is a building with *Aftonhouse Post Office* above it."

That's pretty thin.

"It's just a feeling, Lew. No matter how often I asked, I never found out about his childhood."

Jesus, Dark. It doesn't mean he lived there. It might have been a holiday snap.

"It's the only picture of him I've ever seen. It must be important."

I guess, Lewis agreed. *Like all good con men, Spiral would never allow his picture to be taken.*

"Think, buddy." She stared at the scrap of celluloid, willing it to reveal more "Isn't there anything you can tell me? Something that always puzzled you."

Everything about Spiral puzzled me, Lewis sighed. *You might be heading for more heartache, doll.*

"I loved him, Lew. I need to know what happened. You must understand that?"

There was another long gap.

All right. When we were working together, we liked to use the aliases of silent film stars. But there was one name he always returned to and I'd never heard of him.

Lewis's knowledge of movies was encyclopaedic. If the person were vaguely famous, he would know.

"What was it? I wouldn't be able to pick out an old matinee idol if I was given a mug book."

Frankie Cameron. Pretty similar to the sign in the picture, eh? Lewis sounded perturbed. *I don't imagine Spiral wants to be found, though. Not after disappearing the way he did.*

"What he wants is of little interest to me. I deserve closure."

Listen, Dark. I have no doubt he loved you, so I want you to consider something.

"What's that?"

Spiral was always a dark horse and did his own thing. Suppose he got into serious shit and vanished to protect himself? Or to protect you?

"Then he should have told me. I reckon he was pulling another con, Lew. After promising he'd give that lifestyle up."

How could you possibly know?

"Call it woman's intuition. Listen, it's late, and I'm tired. How about I let you know what I discover?"

Ok, doll. Be safe.

"You too. Goodnight, my friend."

Night, lass. Lovely to hear your voice again.

Lewis hung up.

Dark tossed the photograph onto the floor, pulled the duvet up to her chin and tried to sleep.

She woke to the sound of birds twittering and cows lowing. Somewhere in the distance, she could hear the chug of a tractor.

Dark showered and dressed, then made breakfast in the darkened kitchen. Rubbing her eyes, she finally opened the curtains and threw open the double doors, stepping onto a small wooden landing at the back of the house.

"Fuck me," she breathed. "I'm in a Walt Disney movie."

A stream ran right past the cottage. Behind it was a meadow scattered with flowers and, beyond that, green pastures gave way to sky-scraping mountain peaks. The morning sun bathed the scene in a lambent glow. She sat on a bench, munching toast and sipping coffee from a mug that said *Lairg Folk Festival 1997*.

Frankie Cameron.

She remembered Spiral using the name. Just hadn't thought anything of it before.

Potterrow. Edinburgh 2023

Dark, Spiral and Lewis

Dark drew up outside Potterrow Student Union and parked the white van on a double yellow line, as any real workman would. On either side, in bright red letters, the vehicle bore a logo:

Black Hart Entertainment.

Spiral and Lewis got out and opened the back. Inside was a sturdy trolley and a single arcade game, purchased with cash from a warehouse in Glasgow two weeks before. It had been a cheap buy because it didn't work.

The trio had spent several hours revamping the machine. Lewis fixed the electronics while Spiral and Dark polished the whole thing until it shone.

"Ready, Mr. Cameron?" Lewis pulled a cap down over his eyes, obscuring his face from any CCTV cameras.

"Always, Mr. Valentino." Spiral did the same.

The bar at Potterrow union was almost deserted when they wheeled in the game - a few half-shaven young men reading newspapers and a group of girls talking quietly over coffee. It was Sunday morning and most students were still sleeping off a weekend of partying.

They placed the arcade game next to one that always stood in the corner of the pub. The barman looked across at them without the slightest flicker of interest. Spiral and Lewis manoeuvred their machine to the floor and heaved the existing one onto the trolley. This required some effort, as the union machine was filled with money gambled away by drunken punters the night before. Plus, it was rigged not to pay out.

Spiral took a lump of chewing gum from his mouth and stuck it in the coin slot. Then they began to drag the trolley across the room.

"What are you two doing?"

The pair spun round. A woman in a white blouse and straight skirt was standing behind them, a pile of empty glasses nestled in the crook of one arm.

"Morning, love," Spiral said cheerily. "You the manager?"

"I'm the assistant manager."

"Good enough for me, darling." Spiral waved a clipboard at her. "Bunch of pissheads buggered this machine last night. It's got gum stuck in the coin slot."

The assistant manager peered where he was indicating and grimaced.

"Sorry about that," she said apologetically. "I wasn't on duty."

"Happens all the time, babe." Spiral nodded at the empty game they had just left. "We've put in a replacement. It's not the same type but it ought to do for a few days while we get this one sorted."

He thrust the clipboard at her.

"Can you sign here? Show we've been?"

"Sure. May I have your name for my records?"

"Absolutely. It's Frankie Cameron."

The assistant manager set down the glasses and scribbled her signature at the bottom of the release form.

"Thanks, toots." The two men grabbed the arms of the trolley and staggered towards the exit. The assistant manager held the door open for them.

In the back of the van, they got to work with silent efficiency. Spiral pulled out the chewing gum while it was still soft and took off the front of the slot machine. Lewis used a crowbar to pry open the lock box. They emptied dozens of pound coins into a laundry sack, closed the box and sealed it with superglue. Then they fastened the front back onto the game and set off for the next university union, to repeat the process.

By the end of the afternoon, they had removed the week's takings from over a dozen 'replaced' machines.

"How much do you think we got?" Dark shouted as she drove their van into the countryside.

"Not a bad haul for one afternoon," came the chirpy reply. "I bet there's at least five grand here."

"Betting's a mug's game, Spiral." Dark swerved into an isolated side road and skidded to a halt. Jumping out, she removed the licence plates stolen from an abandoned mini the night before. Spiral pulled out the real ones, hidden under the driver's seat and fastened them in place. Then they peeled away the homemade stickers on the vehicle's sides and crumpled them up.

Both men took off the latex gloves they had worn all day.

"Congratulations on your first con, Dark." Spiral leaned into the cab and kissed her.

"It was certainly a rush," she grinned. "I've come over all Bonny and Clyde."

"You start waving Tommy guns around?" Lewis groaned. "I'm getting out and walking."

"You could do with the exercise," Spiral elbowed him. "But we'll stick to being one-armed bandits. Get it?"

"The managers of those places won't get into trouble, will they?" Dark frowned.

"Nope," Spiral assured her. "Our release forms are genuine. Amazing what you can find on the web."

"And the company who run the gaming machines have plenty of insurance," Colin added. "As well as being dodgy as hell."

"Fair enough." Dark put the van in gear and drove back into town.

Cameron's Store 2024

Dark, Elspeth and Frankie

Frankie Cameron. Dark fetched the faded photograph from the bedroom and checked it again.

Fr. Cameron: Licenced Grocery Store.

Wasn't much of a clue, yet it was all she had. She finished her toast, cleaned up and got into her rented car.

"Time to go tilting at windmills." She put on the Sat-Nav and headed for the village.

Despite the passing of years, Aftonhouse looked much the same as it did in the picture. Not that Dark was surprised, for time seemed to stand still in this part of the world. A hundred yards of neat stone houses lined the road, with a few side streets, leading nowhere, and a small hotel at one end. She parked next to the grocery store and went inside.

A red-headed woman stood behind the counter, reading a magazine. She looked staggered at seeing a stranger, especially one dressed entirely in black. But a friendly smile was quick to emerge.

"Hi there," she said pleasantly. "How can I help you today?"

"This is going to sound weird, but I'm looking for a guy called Frankie Cameron. I'm guessing he might have owned this store once."

"Still does," the woman grinned. "But Frankie is a woman. It's my mum, Frances Cameron."

She put away the magazine.

"Can I ask why you're looking for her?"

"I'm writing a magazine article on the area." Dark had plenty of practice thinking on her feet. "I hoped she might be able to help."

"Mum certainly knows the place well enough." She pressed a buzzer by the till. "We live above the shop, so she'll be down in a minute."

The woman extended her arm.

"I'm Elspeth Cameron."

"Dorothy Arrowsmith." Dark shook her hand. "But friends normally call me Dark. It's a beautiful village."

"Beautiful and a teeny bit boring," Elspeth winked. "Don't put that in your article, though. We need all the trade we can get."

"In that case, I'll have a couple of bottles of Pinot Grigio and a Kit Kat."

"Morning dear," A woman appeared in the doorway behind Elspeth. "Looking for something in particular?"

"This is Dark Arrowsmith, mum. She's a reporter, writing an article about Aftonhouse."

"I don't want to disturb you," Dark said. "But I had a few questions, and your daughter claims you're quite knowledgeable on the subject."

"Is that so? She usually says I'm a pain in the ass."

"Mum!" Elspeth blushed. "Try and be civil for two minutes."

"It takes a lot to tear me away from *Grand Designs* but I've seen this particular episode before." The woman turned and started up the stairs again. "C'mon and we'll have a wee chat. Bring your Kit Kat."

"Make that three bottles, Elspeth." Dark followed her.

Frankie brewed tea in the kitchen while Dark studied the living room. It was filled with steel and glass furniture and kinetic sculptures. Not a flying duck or dusty knick-knack in sight.

"So, you want to write about Aftonhouse Glen," Frankie set down a mug in front of her. On the front were the words *I love to wrap both my hands around it and swallow.*

"I'm looking for a few pointers." Dark immediately liked Frankie Cameron. She must have been in her sixties but was dolled up to the nines, with a pink streak in her hair.

"It's got a ring of standing stones, a 17th-century church, an overgrown battlefield and a curse," the woman continued. "That's all the highlights I can think of off the top of my head."

"Excellent. I didn't know most of that."

"I thought you were doing research?"

"My editor wanted me to pick some remote spot, so I stuck my finger on the map." Dark recovered quickly. "I Googled the place, of course, but there wasn't much information."

"That's Aftonhouse for you," Frankie complained. "The village Scotland's tourist board forgot."

"I'll get the gen on all those things later, if you don't mind." Dark pulled out her mobile. "At the moment, I'm just looking for long-term residents like yourself. People who can fill me in on the history of the place. Who lived here and what they did. That kind of thing."

She pressed a recording app.

"Anyone fit that bill?"

"Melissa McAllister at the post office or old Gordon Crabb would be the best two. I can email you their addresses. And there's Mad Wullie Smith. He's been here forever, but I wouldn't bother asking him."

"Why not?"

"Cause he's mad."

"Fair enough." Dark unwrapped her Kit Kat and offered Frankie a piece. "Y'know, I once overheard a couple of people in Edinburgh talking about Aftonhouse." She kept her voice steady. "They mentioned a guy called Spiral Wood. Ever heard of him?"

For a second, Dark was sure the woman flinched. Then Frankie recovered and laughed out loud.

"I take it you have?" Dark held her breath.

"Sort of. But Spiral Wood isn't a person. It's a place."

"Interesting name." Dark kept her voice neutral. "I might take some pictures of it."

"It's on what used to be the Robertson farm," Frankie said. "The land was sold off years ago, but Lachlan Robertson still has a house there."

"I could ask him for permission?"

"I don't think you need it, though Lachlan could sorely do with some female company. He grew up here but rarely comes into town." She looked sad. "He's a solitary type."

"I'll give it a go." Dark finished her tea. "Listen, this was a flying visit because I only arrived last night. I'm staying at a holiday home a couple of miles away. Can I come and talk to you again once I'm settled in?"

"Of course. As my daughter probably pointed out, there's nothing much else to do around here."

"Thank you so much."

"Pop over any night," the woman said. "If you're getting paid by the word, feel free to bring your wine. I like to talk."

"Is there a Mr. Cameron?" Dark asked. "I could get his input too."

"He died a couple of years ago, I'm afraid."

"Oh. Sorry."

"No need to be, dear. You didn't kill him."

"I almost forgot. There was another name I overheard in that conversation about Aftonhouse. Martin Cindrić? Ring any bells."

"Nope." Frankie shook her head. "He's not local, that's for sure."

"I'll be back, anyhow," Dark promised. "I've got a feeling I'd rather enjoy your stories."

Robertson Farmhouse 2024

Dark and Lachlan

Dark bounced over a potholed lane, following Frankie's directions, until the Robertson property hove into sight. It was a large two-story farmstead with a rutted track leading to a huge barn. The place had a well-kept but simple garden, not much more than a neatly mown lawn. There was a wheelbarrow filled with flowers in the middle and a few potted plants on the windowsills. Behind the building, a wooded hill rose steeply to dominate the skyline. Not firs or pines, but thick, twisted, deciduous trees of various sorts. Dark hadn't a clue what any of them were, but they gave the forest a sinister air - like something from a gothic fairy tale.

She parked a respectable distance away, walked to the front door and knocked. It opened almost immediately. She assumed the occupant had watched her coming.

He was in his late forties, wearing a woolly fleece and sporting a greying beard and shoulder-length hair. Sleepy green eyes regarded her curiously.

"Hi there." Dark waggled her fingers at him. For a few seconds, they stared awkwardly at each other.

"Sorry," he said politely. "Are you… lost?"

"I don't mean to disturb you." Dark quickly switched from friendly to formal. "I'm looking for Lachlan Robertson?"

"That's me."

Robertson was good looking in an unkempt way, though his face seemed made more for scowling than laughing.

"I'm Dark Arrowsmith." She gave a winning smile. "Got your name from Frankie Cameron."

Lachlan nodded but didn't invite her in.

"I'm doing an article on Aftonhouse and interviewing some of the locals." She trotted out her adopted line. "I wondered if I might ask you a few questions."

"I dinnae live in Aftonhouse." Lachlan looked puzzled. "It's five miles east."

"Well, it's the whole glen, really," Dark persisted. "Frankie seemed to think you'd be a good candidate and I came all this way."

"Frankie said that?" The man looked suspicious. "You better come in then. After all, you must have driven a whole six minutes tae get here."

Dark frowned but Lachlan was already ushering her inside.

Like Frankie's flat, the interior of the house was surprising. Modern paintings adorned two walls and a large flat-screen TV took up most of the other. An expensive computer sat on a solid oak desk, sandwiched between two substantial leather couches and a couple of arched silver standing lights. Instead of windows, glass sliding doors opened onto a balcony, so close to the trees she could almost touch them.

"You want a cup of coffee or something?" Lachlan stood behind her, looking flustered. "I dinnae get a lot of company here, so haven't much in the way of snacks."

"Do you have Coke?"

"No, sorry." He thought for a moment. "I've got pear juice."

"I don't think I've ever had pear juice."

"It's juice. Made fae pears."

"That will do fine."

Lachlan retreated to the kitchen. Dark removed her coat, took off her boots and curled up both legs on the couch. Partly because she didn't want to mess up the place. Partly to make it more difficult for him to get rid of her.

"Make yourself at home." Lachlan came back with two glasses. "Ah. You already have."

He placed the drinks on a low table in front of her and sat in a captain's chair next to his desk.

"Writing anything interesting?" Dark leaned across to take a peek at his laptop by his elbow.

"A history of the 19th-century cheese making industry in Ingersoll, Ontario." He shut the lid quickly. "But I cannae decide whether tae approach it chronologically or by individual dairy products."

His face remained impassive.

"Is that a subtle way of telling me to mind my own business?" Dark raised an eyebrow.

"You've a reporter's instinct, sure enough." Lachlan relaxed a little. "Dark. That's an odd handle."

"It's a nickname. I'm actually called Dorothy." She reached out and shook his hand. "Will you answer a few questions?"

"I grew up in Aftonhouse," Lachlan admitted. "I suppose I can tell you the history of the place but I travel quite a bit and just got back from a business trip, so I'm not really up on the latest gossip."

He stroked his beard.

"Where were you this time?" Dark got out her phone.

"Ingersoll," he replied without hesitation. "It's in Canada."

"Involved in the cheesemaking industry, by any chance?"

"You really are good." But he smiled for the first time and it changed his face entirely. Made him look genuinely approachable.

Then it was gone.

"Enough of me. What would you like tae know about Aftonhouse?"

"Can you tell me about Spiral Wood?" Dark took a sip of her drink. It was rich and sweet. "This is nice, by the way. Do you make it yourself?"

Lachlan raised an eyebrow.

"They sell cartons of it in the Oban supermarket."

"Ah." She took another swallow. "Where exactly is Spiral Wood? Frankie said you lived nearby."

Lachlan nodded and pointed. Dark followed the direction with her eyes.

"It's… eh… east of here? Or is that west?"

"It's right outside."

"Closer than I thought." The woman reddened. Some of the branches actually curved over the balcony rail. "If you don't mind me saying, it's a bit creepy."

"Tell me about it. In the middle of the night, it's bloody terrifying." Lachlan smiled again. "Unfortunately, the wood came with the property and I'd probably get intae trouble if I burned it tae the ground."

This time, Dark grinned. She was warming to his deadpan sense of humour.

"It's a rather weird name. Any reason for it?"

"It's officially Clachan Hill but the locals have always called it Spiral Wood cause of the twisty old trees. It's supposed tae be haunted, not that it deterred you."

"That's cause I didn't know." She raised her glass to him. "Anyway, I'm a persistent bugger. One of my few good qualities."

"It has a curse as well."

"Which is exactly the sort of thing I'm looking for!" Dark enthused. She pressed record on her phone, forgetting for a second that being an article writer was just her cover.

"You want the long or short version?" Lachlan asked.

"Short for now. My readers have the attention span of boiled cabbage."

"Long ago, let's say about the 1400s, because I've nae idea of the real date." Lachlan settled back in his seat. "There was tae be a wedding between the rich Laird's son and a beautiful young peasant woman."

"Laird is like a Scottish Lord, yeah?"

"Aye. But the son died the day before in a freak accident. His fiancée was so distraught she persuaded an enchantress to turn her into a white doe and her dead lover into a black hart. That's a male deer."

Lachlan shrugged.

"The sorceress didn't know that the girl and her fiancé had promised not to meet before the wedding. So, they haunt Spiral Wood tae this day - but the hart must stay on one side of the hill and the doe on the other."

"Pretty sad."

"They were none too pleased aboot it and, over the centuries, their bitterness increased. So, being magical creatures, they cursed the place."

He leaned forwards, his voice a whisper.

"Legend has it that any lovers who venture near Spiral Wood are doomed."

"You don't say," Dark grunted. "Carry on."

Couples still dinnae go there, even today. You know how superstitious highland folk are."

"But you live here."

"I also live in the 21ˢᵗ century. Besides, I'm alone and not in love."

"Awesome! I'll certainly be using that." Dark switched off her app. "I'd still like to know more about you, though. Bit of background if you like."

"I write about cheese and watch a lot of Netflix while I'm doing it. Keep myself tae myself."

"Isn't that… lonely?"

"It is, though I dinnae mind. I should but I dinnae." He looked at her evenly. "What about you?"

"Me?"

"Yeah. You seem a… questioning type. And not just because of the job." He gave a chortle. "You're very good at putting people at ease. However, I sense that took some practice rather than being natural."

"So long as it works, eh?" His perceptiveness almost caught Dark off guard. "Have I put *you* at ease?"

"You have. Though I still prefer stories tae talking aboot myself."

"Can I suggest a compromise?" Dark put away her phone and made a spontaneous decision. "I saw the hotel in Aftonhouse has a restaurant and bar. Let me take you to dinner tomorrow night. Then it's not an interview. It's a conversation."

"You're that bored, eh?"

"You seem a decent enough guy," Dark admitted. "But yes. I've only been here one day and it's not what I'm used to. Didn't realise I'd become such a city girl."

"Well, dinnae ask the locals where you can go clubbing," Lachlan deadpanned. "Or they'll take you oot tae kill rabbits."

"Noted." Dark squinted at him. "I didn't honestly think you'd say yes."

"I'm not the most sociable person in the world but I'm not a hermit either." He spread his hands wide. "Truth is, it's rare to find someone who actually wants tae hear the fascinating history of Canadian cheeses."

"Did I say that?"

"It's a deal-breaker, I'm afraid."

"Then my enthusiasm knows no bounds." Dark pulled on her boots. "Shall we say eight o clock?"

"I'll meet you there." He escorted her to the door "Dinnae wear a tartan dress or I'll never be able tae find you."

"I'm not sure what you mean."

"You will when you get a look at the wallpaper."

"I like that the place is cursed," Dark said. "Readers lap this kind of thing up."

"Oh, aye. There's never a dull moment here." Lachlan waved goodbye as Dark walked to her car, then shut the door. In the background, Spiral Wood loomed over the building, exuding a palpable air of menace.

Dark shuddered and drove away. Lachlan watched her from the window.

"Cursed?" he said softly. "You don't know the half of it. I lost my best friend, the woman I loved and my whole bloody family here."

Robertson Farm 1993

Lachlan, Helen and Archie

"Damn!" Helen Robertson stared at the distant clouds. "There's a snowstorm coming. A big one, by the looks of it."

"Cool!" Lachlan's little brother, Archie, was too young to appreciate the danger. "Will we be caught?"

"Not if I can help it. Get in the land buggy."

At 17, Lachlan was old enough to spot the fear in his mother's voice. And he'd lived in Aftonhouse long enough to understand the reason. They were at the furthest reaches of the Robertson farm, looking for stray sheep. It had been a harsh winter and the ground was layered with thin drifts. The trio were well insulated, wearing padded jackets, fur hats and gloves - and the buggy was big enough not to get bogged down. But if they were caught in a whiteout, visibility would be reduced to zero.

"C'mon tiny." He hoisted his brother into the vehicle. "Let's race it."

"We'll come back for this. It'll slow us down too much." His mother unhitched the empty sheep trailer, jumped into the driver's seat and roared off.

She wound her way between forbidding white hills, sticking to the floor of the valley, while Lachlan kept his eyes on the darkening sky behind them.

"Careful, mum," he cautioned. "We'll outrun the storm but not if we end up hitting a boulder."

Helen nodded, concentrating on the terrain ahead. As they entered the next valley, she edged up the incline. The floor of the gorge contained a small loch, iced over and invisible under the snow.

"I shouldn't have brought you both," she muttered under her breath. "What was I thinking?"

"It's fine, mum. You'll make it."

"Faster," Archie squealed. "I love this!"

The buggy's wide tyres and spiked treads held the ground perfectly well at slower speeds. But now the vehicle lurched and slid as the slope steepened. Helen's arms were already aching with the effort of keeping it in a straight line.

She risked a glance over her shoulder to chart the storm's progress.

"Look out!" Lachlan shouted.

A fallen silver birch materialised in front of them. Helen wrenched the steering wheel to the right and slammed on the brake.

The buggy went into a spin, slithering sideways down the hill. It hit the edge of the loch and rolled twice before landing upright. Ice splintered, and the vehicle plunged into the shallow water, until it was up to the occupant's chests.

Lachlan unfastened his seat belt, pulled Archie from the back and carried him to the shore.

"Come on, mum!" he shouted.

"I think I'm hurt," came the mournful reply.

He waded back and helped Helen limp to safety. By the time they reached the bank, their legs were so numb they could no longer stand. Both collapsed in a heap.

"I'm very cold." Archie whimpered, teeth chattering so much he could hardly talk.

Lachlan inspected his mother's shin. The strange angle left him in no doubt it was broken.

"Good job I can't feel it, eh?" she smiled wanly, trying to keep panic from her voice.

Lachlan looked around at the hostile landscape. There was nothing he could salvage from the buggy and no dry wood anywhere to make a fire. Worse, the first flurries of snow were already drifting over the landscape.

Helen had come to the same conclusion.

"We need to huddle together for warmth," she said. "Wait to get rescued."

"Nobody knows we're here, mum. The satellite phone is dead in the loch. When the storm arrives properly, it'll cover us completely. We'll never be found."

Helen gave a strangled sob.

Lachlan thumped his legs to get the circulation flowing. He was wearing waterproof trousers and boots and knew the area well.

"I'm going tae get help," he said. "Gordon Crabbe's house is closest."

"It's almost seven miles!" Helen protested.

"I dinnae have a choice."

"Take your brother," his mother relented. "I'll be fine."

"I'll have to run tae outpace the storm. Archie couldnae walk half that distance in normal conditions."

"Then carry him!"

"If I do that, *I* winnae make it. Anyway, the storm would engulf us long before we got there."

He pushed Archie into his mother's embrace.

"Keep each other warm as best you can.

"Lachlan Roberson!" Helen snapped. "You *will* take your brother."

"You cannae leave me behind, Lachie," the boy wailed. "That's not fair. Mum always says we have tae look oot for each other."

Lachlan glanced at the other end of the valley. Already, the furthest peaks were lost in a swirling vortex. Every second counted.

He began to cry.

"Stop that," Helen commanded. "Take your brother and go. Now!"

"I'll try and be light," Archie promised, reaching out a hand. "I winnae wriggle."

"I know you don't understand." The boy straightened up and took a deep breath. "But this is our only chance."

Then he ran

"Lachie!" his brother wailed in terror. "Come back!"

"Don't you dare leave him!" Helen screamed. "Lachlan Robertson! Don't do this! Get back here, you bloody coward!"

She kept shrieking until her voice was hoarse and her eldest son was a speck in the distance.

Bruntsfield Links, Edinburgh 2023

Dark, Spiral and Nancy

The memento box was a little oasis, offering an odd sort of comfort in an unfamiliar place. Dark opened it before she got into bed, shut her eyes and rummaged around until her hand fastened on an object. She pulled out a little charm bracelet. Attached to it was a locket with **N** inscribed on the surface. It was a cheap trinket, no more than a child's thing. Still, she fastened it to her wrist for the night.

Like everything else in the box, it was a memory made physical.

Dark and Spiral Wood were on their way home to his house after the pub closed. It was a beautiful summer night and, even at this time of the morning, the temperature was pleasant. They crossed the Meadows, then Bruntsfield Links.

"Golf is supposed to have been invented here." Spiral waved his arm around the park. "By James IV of Scotland."

"Did Lewis tell you that, perchance?"

"Nah. I'm good pals with Sean Connery. Plus, it's written on a plaque over there."

Between the links and Spiral's apartment was a stretch of ultra-posh houses with walled, tree-lined gardens.

"Let's go into one of these," Dark whispered.

"I'm not sure I'm ready to graduate to burglary." Spiral pulled a face. "After all I've drunk, I'd probably fall down the stairs."

"Just the garden," Dark giggled. "It's not *their* valuables I want to get my hands on."

"Oh," he grinned. "What a fine idea."

They quietly opened one wooden gate and crept through. The lights in the house were out, so they felt their way until they found a large patch of lawn.

Dark pulled off her tights while Spiral unfastened his belt. He silently lowered himself on top of her.

"That OK?"

"Oh, yeah."

He began to move backwards and forwards, his rhythm getting faster and faster. Dark grabbed his hair with one hand and held the other over her mouth, to stop herself from crying out. She wrapped her boots around his waist and thrust against him as he groaned.

"Ready?" he hissed.

"Oh, fuck, yes. Yes! Spiral... I'm coming!"

As always, they climaxed at the same time, bodies shuddering with the intensity of the moment. Spiral rolled over and sprawled on his back, panting and laughing breathlessly.

"I'll never get the grass stains out of my jeans."

"Shit... I hope the folk in that house are heavy sleepers," Dark giggled. "That was fun, though."

"Yeah, it was. And there's a whole street to go. Y'know I..."

"Spiral!" Dark sat up. "Somebody is watching us!"

"What? Where?" Spiral quickly pulled the jeans over his butt. "Who's there?"

"Me." A torch went on and a girl's face was illuminated a few feet away.

She was sitting under the closest tree, wearing a thick floral nightgown, and couldn't have been more than fourteen years old.

"Fuck me," Spiral recovered quickly. "I just about shat myself. What are you *doing* here?"

"This is where I live," the girl replied awkwardly.

"Where? In the shed?"

"We're sorry," Dark apologised. "We haven't done any damage. Honestly."

"Don't worry, my parents won't wake up." The girl didn't seem afraid. "You could've had a Roman orgy, and they wouldn't have stirred."

"Why are you sitting in the garden?" Spiral asked. "It's two in the morning."

"I'm… depressed." The girl tuned her flashlight on them.

"Hold on." Spiral struggled into a kneeling position and pulled up his zip. "OK. That was *definitely* something you shouldn't have witnessed."

"I didn't mean to disturb you."

"That's OK. We're finished."

"We were on our way home from the pub," Dark said. "And thought it would be romantic to do it under the stars."

She squinted into the beam.

"Eh. We don't have a garden, you see. Just a tennis court."

"And it's floodlit," Spiral added.

"You picked a nice spot," the girl nodded, looking around.

"I think introductions might be in order. I'm Spiral and this is Dark. Weird names, I know."

"I'm Nancy."

"Want a cigarette?"

"Spiral!" Dark punched him.

"Of course not." Spiral fumbled in his pockets and lit one of his own. "So, Nancy. Depressed, is it?"

"Yes," the girl replied miserably.

"Could you put the torch out before a plane lands?" Spiral looked nervously at the house. "We can chat in the dark."

Nancy switched off the flashlight and the garden was plunged into shadow, except for a red dot on the end of Spiral's cigarette.

"What does a youngster like you have to be fed up about?" he asked. "Apart from that nightgown, which I only got a glimpse of, but I'm pretty sure your mum bought."

"I don't know where to start." The girl hesitated. "It doesn't matter anyway."

"Sometimes strangers are the best people to talk to, especially when you can't see them. Like a help line." Spiral's voice dipped. "We're here now and we're not in a hurry, are we, Dark?"

"Not anymore."

"Get comfortable and start with your mum and dad. It's usually a good beginning." Spiral took a long drag. "That and school."

"My parents are nice people," Nancy said. "But... God. Really dull, I know that sounds bad."

"Not at all. Your opinion is valid."

"My life is boring and proper. I'm ugly and dumb, and it's never gonna change." The floodgates seemed to have opened. "I'll probably get married to some guy with a double-breasted suit and hair like a brillo pad and end up working at the T.S.B. in Morningside Road."

"And school?" Dark joined in.

"Hate it."

"You're certainly eloquent enough," Spiral said. "Is the garden where you do your deep thinking?"

"I was thinking about ending it all," Nancy sniffed. "My parents would be mortified if I topped myself in the house."

"Seems like nothing will ever change, eh?" Spiral's voice had softened even more. "Then again, you never know what will happen."

He stubbed out his cigarette.

"May I tell you a short story?"

"I suppose."

"I once saw a bunch of aliens."

"There's no need to take the piss," Nancy bristled.

"I'm not, I assure you." Spiral objected. "Think of it as a parable. You know what a parable is?"

"Yeah. My parents sent me to Sunday School. I hated that too."

"OK, then. I was hill walking up north, trying to get a photo of the Great Eel of Loch Awe, when I bumped into them trying to fix their flying saucer. It was parked behind the betting shop at Drumnadrochit."

"I haven't heard this one," Dark side. "Do go on."

"I gave them a hand to get it started. A good hard kick and it worked fine."

Spiral took out another cigarette and handed one to Dark. She assumed he was stalling while he tried to think up an ending to his tale.

"As a reward, they wanted me to come with them," Spiral continued. "Said I was destined for great things. Guess they really were impressed with my spaceship starting skills. They promised I'd see a thousand amazing civilizations and never go bald."

Nancy laughed quietly at this. Spiral had the gift of comic timing.

"I asked if I could bring anyone with me but they said no. Apparently, it wasn't the done thing."

He lit the cigarettes.

"So, I thought and thought and, eventually, I said: *All right, just let me say goodbye to Dark and tell her why I won't be coming back.*"

"They said: *Dark? That's a stupid name.*"

"You gave it to me," The woman snorted. "What a cheek."

"Especially since they were called Sporg and Mogwodron," Spiral agreed. "Anyhoo, they said no again. I think aliens have a lot of rules. They insisted I come right there and then and nobody could ever know what happened to me."

"What did you do?" Even Dark was intrigued.

"I asked them... What's the point in doing great things if nobody knows I did them? Can you guess what they said?"

"No?"

"*Why should you care? You'll be dead. Besides, you're not going to amount to much in this podunk backwater.* I presume they meant earth and not just Drumnadrochit."

He smiled thinly, like some weird Cheshire cat, his lips the only thing illuminated by the ashen glow.

"So, I told *them* no. I'd take my chances here. Better a pointless, lonely life of my own than just being a vehicle for someone else's hopes and dreams."

He shuffled closer to Nancy.

"I got a photo of the great eel of Loch Awe too, but my thumb was over the lens. And the aliens gave me a little bit of their hair as a keepsake. Odd stuff. It looks like mangy fur."

He took another puff.

"They were going to kill me to keep their existence secret at first. Then they realised nobody would believe me."

He held the cigarette out to the girl.

"Nobody ever does."

"I know the feeling." Nancy shook her head. "I'll pass, thank you."

"Quite right." Spiral took it back. "No sense in shortening your life."

He put his arm around Dark.

"Don't ever think that loneliness can't be borne, Nancy. One day, it will either fade away or you'll make it your friend."

He stood up, pulling Dark with him.

"When you go to school on Monday, pick a fight with the person you dislike most. You'll win, or they'll win. Either way, you'll be on your path to feeling free."

"I didn't understand most of what you just told me," Nancy admitted.

"Parables are like that," Spiral shrugged. "Just something to ponder. But I want you to do me a favour."

"What?"

"Shag someone in this garden one day, even if your parents don't live here anymore. It'll mean you remember us."

"Spiral!" Dark slapped his arm.

"I'll keep that in mind." The girl smiled and stood as well. "I'm going in now."

On impulse, she took a small bracelet from her wrist and handed it to Spiral.

"So you'll remember me too."

"I promise not to let Dark steal it. You be well, kid." Spiral took his companion's hand and led her away.

She turned on him once they were out on the street.

"What the hell was that little speech all about?"

"Sometimes, young people just need to be listened to. See their doubts and fears warrant more than a pat reply."

He kissed her.

"So what if it doesn't make any sense?"

That's when Dark sensed she might be falling in love with Spiral Wood.

Aftonhouse Restaurant 2024

Dark and Lachlan

Dark spent all day exploring the glen. She'd considered visiting the Camerons again but figured it was too soon. She found a little church and lost count of the number of highland cows she spotted. Yet the area around Aftonhouse village was pretty much deserted. She even went to the battlefield, but there was nothing there except a small car park, a ploughed field and a sign. She took a few pictures for something to do, then drove home to get changed.

There was no need for her to write any article. After all, it had just been a con to help her track down Spiral. Yet, she decided she would. The idea of being a writer had always appealed to her and now she had a good excuse. She might even be able to sell it to a real magazine.

But there was more to it than that.

Part of her didn't want to let Frankie Cameron down.

Dark managed to find a local taxi driver who could take her to Aftonhouse village and back so she didn't have to drive. She wasn't entirely sure if this dinner with Lachlan Robertson would be a pleasure or an ordeal. Either way, she felt alcohol would smooth things over.

The hotel was quaint to the point of caricature, with a horse-drawn cart and a couple of whisky barrels outside. She walked into the restaurant and asked for a table.

There weren't many people and every head turned to stare at her. She was an obvious stranger, dressed in a short satin dress with her trademark black tights and boots.

She sat down and looked around, immediately understanding Lachlan's comment about her attire. The wallpaper was tartan and so were the curtains and tablecloths. A couple of deer heads adorned the walls and there was a small bar in one corner.

The door opened and Lachlan entered. He had abandoned his woollen fleece and wore a shirt with a silk tie under a black dress leather jacket. It looked expensive. All in all, he was rather presentable, Dark thought, like a slightly faded film star, trying to seem trendy and almost pulling it off.

"Did you order wine?" He sat down opposite her.

"Not yet."

"Dinnae ask for the house special. It tastes like someone watered the stuff wi sheep dip." He thought for a second. "Actually, that might well be true."

"I'll let you pick. I like dry white."

"Can we have a couple of menus and a bottle of Seven Oaks?" Lachlan asked the waitress. "Do you have a vegetarian option?"

"We've got chips." She shot Dark a worried look. "You're no a vegan, are you? Mah aunt was wan of those. Angry woman. Used tae shout at the butcher's van."

"It's for me," Lachlan said patiently.

"Oh. I'll check with the chef."

When she was gone, he stuck his bottom teeth over his top lip.

"Get stared at by the locals when you came in?" he lisped. "Oooh, look. A stranger fae the big smoke. I hear they have Sushi bars there. Run by mad transvestites."

"Aren't you a local, too?" Dark smiled.

"Aye. And they're decent people." Lachlan looked abashed. "I was just trying tae appear cosmopolitan."

"You don't have to. I was brought up in a small Australian town. Didn't put on a pair of shoes till I was sixteen."

"I'm hoping that's an exaggeration. I dinnae want you swinging fae the lights like Cheetah once you've had a couple of glasses."

"Shame. I can hold on just using my toes."

"There's an image that's going tae haunt me for the rest of my life."

The waitress brought the wine and poured each a glass. They ordered and waited until she had gone.

"So?" Dark said. "Tell me about Ingersoll. I'm all ears."

"It was a 19th-century bloke called James McIntyre who first sparked my interest. He was born in Forres, up north and emigrated to Canada at the age of fourteen. He worked as a hired hand, became a furniture dealer, then established a factory in Ingersoll, Ontario - the heart of Canada's dairy and cheese making provinces."

"I'm rivetted so far," Dark yawned.

"It was in there that McIntyre found his vocation, publishing two volumes of collected poems: *Musings on the Banks of Canadian Thames* and *Poems of James McIntyre*."

"You moved swiftly on to art. A nice transition."

"I'm oot tae impress." Lachlan grinned. "At first, McIntyre's poetry covered a variety of topics, albeit badly. Patriotism, Canadian authors, Ontario towns, rural life, foreign wars, poets, philosophers and morality were all grist for his grating poetic mill. His obsession, however, was cheese."

Lachlan rolled his eyes.

"He wrote volumes of dairy verse that transcended mere dreadfulness - though it earned him the rather flattering title *The Chaucer of Cheese*. It's unclear just why he placed cheese above all other subjects, or even above other dairy products, But McIntyre's verse manages tae convey something close tae worship."

"You're making this up!" Dark giggled.

"I'll Google it if you dinnae believe me." He got out his mobile and tapped the keys. "Here we go. *Ode on the Mammoth Cheese (Weight over seven thousand pounds).*"

He read from the screen.

We have seen thee, queen of cheese,
Lying quietly at your ease,
Gently fanned by evening breeze,
Thy fair form no flies dare seize.

All gaily dressed soon you'll go
To the great Provincial show,
To be admired by many a beau
In the city of Toronto.

Cows numerous as a swarm of bees,
Or as the leaves upon the trees,
It did require to make thee please.
And stand unrivalled, queen of cheese.

May you not receive a scar as
We have heard that Mr. Harris
Intends to send you off as far as
Folks would think it was the moon
About to fall and crush them soon.

"You are shitting me!" Dark almost choked on her drink.

"Pretty hard tae beat, eh?"

"You remind me of a guy I used to know." Dark filled her glass again. "Lewis. Wonderful man and a master of useless facts."

She looked at her companion evenly.

"You've never been to Ingersoll, have you? And you're not writing about it either."

"No," Lachlan confessed. "I like poetry, though. And cheese. Does that count?"

"But you don't like talking about yourself. I get it."

"Not for a magazine article. I'm quite a private person."

The food arrived and gave them a few seconds respite as they tucked in.

"I propose a truce," Dark said. "I've had a rough time over the last few months and wouldn't want anyone poking into that."

"Care tae tell me? Or is that the very definition of poking?"

"Not right now. But I could do with a friend. How about we just talk? I give my word I won't use your name or print anything you say unless it's specifically about the history of Aftonhouse."

She took a forkful of her pasta.

"This is delicious, by the way."

"It's a deal." Lachlan poured them another glass each. "What do you want tae know?"

"You can start with why you live in the middle of nowhere. You don't act like a typical recluse."

"My parents bought a farm up here but my mum died young and dad sold most of it off." He sat back. "All except the house and a few acres around it, including a couple of cottages and Spiral Wood. When my father died, I inherited it. It's my home and my workplace."

"What do you do there?"

"You notice a big barn next tae where I live?"

"Hard to miss."

"That's my workshop."

"You're not Santa, are you?" She speared a lump of broccoli. "I always wanted to meet an elf."

"I'm a sculptor. We're supposed tae live in isolation, aren't we? Besides, this place is beautiful."

"A sculptor," Dark whistled. "That's different. Why didn't you tell me before?"

"It's not something I advertise." Lachlan looked fairly embarrassed. "But it gives me an excuse to travel. Now and then, I go on a tour of art galleries in Europe tae see what ideas I can nick."

He put on an innocent face.

"I mean… tae get some inspiration."

"By yourself?"

"I'm used tae my own company."

"Can I see some of your stuff?"

"I suppose so." He looked at her evenly. "Your turn."

"Struggling writer," Dark said. "Apparently adroit at describing herself in one sentence."

"Try a few longer sentences. You might enjoy it."

Dark had long ago learned that a good con artist incorporated as much truth as they could into their delivery without giving away specifics. And she was adept.

"I was living with a man," she said. "We were in love, or so I assumed. I thought we'd settle down and get married. Then he ran out on me and I've no idea why."

Lachlan stayed silent.

"I want closure. I haven't got it. I'm pissed off and now I don't know what to do with myself."

"The guy was a fool." Lachlan cocked his head at her. "You're fun, interesting, lively and very pretty."

He held up his hands disarmingly.

"Before you get all defensive, it's not a come on and I'm not blowing smoke up your ass. Just showing I can sum you up in one sentence too."

He winked at her.

"I'm very competitive."

They finished their meal and passed on dessert in favour of more wine. They talked easily, drifting through politics, literature, TV and anything else that came into their heads. Lachlan was droll but passionate, reserved yet amusing. Dark was surprised at how well she got on with him. Better than anyone since…

But she couldn't think like that.

A message bleeped on her phone and she glanced at it.

"My taxi has arrived," she said regretfully. "I've had a nice night, though."

"Drop by and see my workshop," Lachlan finished his glass. "I'll make sure the elves stay in their cages. Nasty wee shits, they are."

"I will. Let me just pay for the meal."

"Dinnae be silly." He waved her away. "You get your cab and I'll deal with this."

"Will you be all right to drive?"

"Nae need. I came on a sled pulled by reindeer."

Dark gave a tipsy laugh and left before she did something stupid.

Like suggesting she go home with him for a nightcap.

Spiral's Flat, Edinburgh 2024

Dark and Spiral

Dark got undressed, feeling a little drunk. As usual, she dipped into the memento box, pulling out the first thing that came to hand. It was a small square of fur. She had no idea if it came from an animal or was synthetic but didn't suppose it mattered.

That had been her first clue that something was off about Spiral's disappearance. He might have abandoned her but he wouldn't have left his box of knick-knacks unless he intended to return. She understood that much about him.

Only, he hadn't come back.

Dark put the fur on the pillow beside her head and folded both hands over her chest. As always, sleep was held at bay by memories.

Dark and Spiral lay naked on the bed, spent and soaked with sweat. Dark propped her head up on one elbow and studied her companion. Spiral wasn't particularly tall, but he was broad, with a hairy chest, muscular torso and slim waist. He had a good body, she thought for the hundredth time. Compact, that was how she would describe him. With his lively eyes, even features and short cropped hair, he was handsome. No. Not handsome, so much as sexy. He had sex appeal. That was it.

She rolled onto her stomach and let out a sigh of contentment. He had a comfy bed too.

Spiral inched himself up her body, kissing her back. Despite being from Australia, she was alabaster white, with a rash of freckles across her shoulders. She groaned and pushed her butt against him, moving the pillows to get more comfortable. She squealed as something hairy brushed her hand.

"What the hell is this?" She held up the offending object.

"It's my lucky piece of alien fur. I found it in the cupboard and I'm trying to decide what to do with it."

"I suppose binning the thing is out of the question?" Dark screwed up her face. "Is this the scungy object you had sewn on the crotch of your jeans when I first met you?"

"It was on my knee." He snatched the tatty bit of pelt back and held it lovingly to his cheek. "You can't throw things like this away. They're more reliable than memories."

"I'll bet that conjures up a whole bunch of memories," Dark laughed. "You should stick it in a can of tuna for added effect."

"That's fucking horrible" Spiral's indignity was tinged with amusement.

"Want me to glue it on your receding hairline?"

"I should get a memento box for all my trinkets." Spiral patted his head. "Is my hair honestly receding?"

"There's something very childish about you," Dark ruffled his shorn locks.

"I think the word you're searching for is 'childlike'. Personally, I prefer mature. Or hunky."

"If you say so," Dark smiled. "But you do remind me of a kid waiting to grow up."

Spiral looked at her quizzically.

"You're afraid all the things you want will have vanished by the time you're old enough to get them," Dark continued. "Or they won't live up to your expectations. So, you refuse to get excited about anything big. Concentrate on the little pleasures instead. Except, they're *too* little."

She pulled a cigarette from the packet on the bedside table and fished around for the lighter.

"And when major stuff comes along, it's no better because you won't let it mean anything."

She lit her cigarette.

"I imagine it's like living your life with the mute button always on."

"Where did *that* come from?" Spiral sat up.

"I tend to get reflective after good sex."

"How's this for a big thing, then?" He reached for his own cigarette. "What about you and I going out together? Properly. Think it would work?"

"What? Boyfriend and girlfriend?" Dark looked stunned. "You wouldn't be able to stand it."

"Suppose that's what I wanted. What would you say?"

"I'd say yes."

"Really?" He plonked an ashtray on the bed.

"I'd even live with you, if you asked."

"Seriously?"

"I'd give it a try." She rolled over and tapped his forehead. "Still, I thought you'd rather eat pre-chewed carrots than get all monogamous."

"I never felt like this about anyone," Spiral said. "Though, I don't know why you'd feel the same about me."

"You know that persona you think you've built?" Dark took a drag and blew out a smoke ring. "The fun and carefree one that's supposed to cover up you being a selfish, unfaithful, immature, unfeeling bastard?"

"Yeah."

"It works."

"I don't know what to say."

"That's what I was talking about, you goofball. You pluck up the courage to tackle something like this and have no idea where to take it." She got up and fetched wine and two glasses. "We'll keep things the way we are."

Dark poured them each a drink and handed a glass to Spiral.

"To love at all is to be vulnerable." Spiral closed his eyes and recited. "Love anything, and your heart will certainly be wrung and possibly be broken. If you want to make sure of keeping it intact, you must give your heart to no one. Wrap it carefully round with hobbies and little luxuries; avoid all entanglements; lock it up safe in the casket or coffin of your selfishness. But in that casket - safe, dark, motionless, airless - it will change. It will not be broken; it will become unbreakable, impenetrable, irredeemable."

"Who said that?" Dark was properly moved.

"C.S. Lewis. Wonderful writer. Failed his driving test seventeen times, though."

"Sounds like something my dad would quote."

"What?" Spiral looked worried. "Am I some kind of substitute father figure?"

"I hope not." Dark smiled sadly. "Like my father, however, I sometimes wonder if you know the difference between being alive and feeling alive."

"Just that one of them had the Bee Gees in it." A lost look crossed Spiral's face. "I don't mind something steady. I'm a creature of habit. I just got into the habit of sleeping around."

"Lewis told me one of the Bee Gees was married to Lulu."

"Maurice, I think."

"Who's Lulu?"

"Thing is," Spiral said. "I love you."

Dark bit her lip.

"And I you," she replied.

"You think it would work?" Spiral sipped his drink. "I'd like it to work."

"It doesn't matter," Dark sighed at his hesitancy. "I'm not asking you to settle down, so take the look of panic off your face."

"No. Let's give it a go." Spiral downed his drink. "You and me."

"Maybe you should hold off on the vino."

"It's just that things get old. They lose their magic."

"There isn't enough magic in the world to misplace even a little, I guess."

"I want to build a wall around the way we are." Spiral nuzzled her neck. "But then all you can see is the wall."

"It's fine. We're good."

"The wall and you? To be honest, that's enough for me." He clinked his glass against hers. "You should get your things out of the crappy place where you stay and move in here."

"You really *do* mean it?"

"With all my heart."

"OK." Dark kissed him on the lips. "I'm in."

Despite the wine, Dark still couldn't sleep. She switched on the light, padded to the box of mementos in the corner of the living room and opened it. She rummaged around and pulled out a worn copy of *The Great Gatsby*. Spiral loved C.S. Lewis but F. Scott Fitzgerald was his favourite.

She opened it and flicked through the pages.

Spiral had underlined two passages.

If personality is an unbroken series of successful gestures, then there was something gorgeous about him.

And another near the end

He had come a long way to this blue lawn and his dream must have seemed so close that he could hardly fail to grasp it. He did not know that it was already behind him.

"Is that how you saw yourself?" Dark whispered. "Is that how you saw me? Was I really your dream?"

She closed the book.

"And then you woke up?"

Lachlan was awake too. He sat in the dark at his desk, glass of port in hand, staring at the balcony. He had thoroughly enjoyed his dinner with Dark and that worried him. He couldn't get involved. If experience had taught him anything it was to shun closeness. The people he cared about died or vanished and it had to be more than just coincidence.

Finally, he opened the laptop. The screen lit up his face, turning his eye sockets into sinister hollows. Lachlan stroked his chin and then clicked on a file.

It was an untitled Word document, a short list he had made. He thought for a minute and added Dark's name with a question mark.

CONNECTIONS

Dark Arrowsmith?
Billy Milne.
Ewa Jakubowicz.
Big Don Milne.
Elspeth and Frankie Cameron.
Merchiston Point.

The Big White Truck.

-Part II-

Had I the heavens' embroidered cloths,
Enwrought with golden and silver light,
The blue and the dim and the dark cloths
Of night and light and the half-light,
I would spread the cloths under your feet:
But I, being poor, have only my dreams;
I have spread my dreams under your feet;
Tread softly because you tread on my dreams.
W.B. Yeats. *He Wishes for the Cloths of Heaven*

Lachlan's House 2023

Lachlan and Billy

The big white truck pulled up outside Lachlan Robertson's house. Billy Milne waited in the cab until his friend stepped out. Lachlan had a leather bag slung over one shoulder and a hunting rifle in his hand. He climbed into the passenger side.

"Really?" Billy raised an eyebrow. "We're not driving to the OK Corral."

"I've got a licence for it."

"What's in the satchel? Hand grenades?"

"Sandwiches." Lachlan slid the gun down the side of his seat. "Rifle's not loaded, Bill. It never is."

"Why, bring it then?"

"Intimidation purposes. You haven't asked me to come on a job for years, so something's up."

"Aw, this one couldn't be simpler." Billy put the vehicle in gear. "We drive to Murray's Cove and meet a boat there. Take a walk while they unload the cargo, stow it away and sail into the sunset."

He turned onto the main road.

"When we come back to the truck, there's going to be a suitcase of money on the front seat. Then we head home. Simple as that. No firepower required."

"So, why do you need me? And how come one of your father's regular lackeys didnae make the trip? Young Div or one of Muir Twins?"

"Dad drove up and handed me the keys this morning." Billy hunched over the wheel, making sure to stay just under the speed limit. "He stressed this was pretty important and involved a lot of cash. I guess he didn't trust anyone but me with that much temptation."

He winked at his companion.

"And the only person *I* trust is my best buddy."

"I thought I made it clear, long ago, I didnae do this kind of thing anymore."

He squinted at his companion.

"Come clean, Bill, or let me out."

Billy hesitated.

"I'm not sure the operation was my father's idea," he admitted. "Or me driving the truck, for that matter. I think he was pressured into it."

"The Laird?" Lachlan snorted laughter. "Nobody tells him what tae dae."

The Laird was Billy's father, Big Don Milne. A local smuggler with a thuggish face and personality to match.

"Yeah, yeah, I know. Big Don isn't scared of anyone. But he was frightened when he asked me, I swear."

Billy's hands tightened on the wheel.

"I can't fuck this up, pal. I need my best mate with me. Someone who's always calm and collected."

"I'm still here, aren't I?" Lachlan turned in his seat. "What's the cargo?"

"I've no idea and don't want to know." Billy's face was set in a grim line. "It *seems* simple."

"The fact that you're trying tae snap the steering wheel in half tells me different."

"You know me too well, Lachie." Billy glanced at his white knuckles. "This feels pretty off, know? It's so different from our normal routine."

"But you agreed, anyway."

"The local cops have been bribed to turn a blind eye if that's what you're worried about."

"I'm worried aboot you getting in over your head."

"So am I," Billy said miserably.

"Then, let's not bullshit each other. I dinnae want tae sound mean but your father's never had a lot of faith in you."

"That's putting it mildly."

"Yet he suddenly sticks you in charge of a major operation?"

"Apparently, the client asked specifically I be the driver and that I come alone." Billy wiped a bead of sweat from his brow. "I'm not stupid, Lachie. I can guess the reason. If this goes tits up, who better to hold to ransom than the Laird's son?"

"And Don went *along* with this?"

"Like I said." Billy scratched his lip. "He seemed scared."

"If you're meant tae be alone, what am I going tae do? Pretend tae be a hood ornament?"

"I'll let you off just before I get there. You can keep an eye on things with your telescopic sight thingie."

"Still annoyed I brought the rifle?"

"No. You're a good man in a crisis."

"I'll keep you out of trouble. I always have." Lachlan dipped into his bag. "You want cheese and pickle or tuna and cucumber?"

Maclennan Cottage, Aftonhouse 2024

Belle and Alasdair

The next day, Dark drew up in front of Lachlan's house. He was putting a large plastic container into the back of his car. She got out and strolled over.

"I came to see the workshop. Tried phoning first, but there was no answer."

"It's on silent. I don't get a lot of calls." He shut the boot. "I'm just going out."

"Anywhere interesting?"

"Delivering shopping tae my mother's friends – Belle and Alasdair Maclennan. They're getting on, so I try tae help them a bit when I'm around."

"Doesn't the Oban supermarket deliver?"

"They regard supermarkets as the devil's crowbar," Lachlan snorted. "Live in fear of a giant Ikea warehouse being built over their garden."

"Hmmm. Do they know anything about Aftonhouse and its history?"

"You dinnae want tae come, trust me."

"Oh." Dark's face fell. "OK, then."

"Honestly." Lachlan spotted her crestfallen look. "I mean it. You *really* dinnae want tae."

"Please?" Dark batted her eyelids at him.

"Aw, what the hell. Follow me in your car, then. In case you have tae make a quick escape."

"That bad?"

"You have nae idea."

Ten minutes later, Dark was speeding along the B45 behind Lachlan's Volvo.

They arrived at a small, immaculately kept bothy. The door opened before the cars had even ground to a halt. A tiny woman in a print dress spilled out and hobbled towards him.

"Lachie! How lovely to see you." Her beady eyes wheeled round to Dark. "And who is this?"

"This is Dark, Aunty Belle. She's a reporter fae Edinburgh."

"Oooh!" The woman wheeled round in panic and whizzed back the way she had come, patting her unkempt bun into place. "I better tidy up."

"There's absolutely nae need," Lachlan opened his boot and hauled out the plastic box. "We're just dropping off some groceries."

She was already inside. Lachlan carried the supplies through the hall.

"In here!" the woman called, and they entered the kitchen. A large man with a protruding stomach sat at the table, reading the *Daily Mail*. He wore a tatty pullover and wispy white hair stuck straight up from a wide, shiny forehead, giving the impression he was horrified to see them.

"Hi, Uncle Alasdair." Lachlan put the groceries on a tiled counter. "This is Dark."

"Dark, is it?" the man grunted. "That's a bizarre name."

"It's short for Darkmella," Lachlan replied before his companion could explain.

"Sounds foreign." Suspicion clouded the man's face.

"I'm Australian."

"Hmmm. I seen *Crocodile Dundee* once." The man went back to his newspaper. "It was rubbish."

"Would you like a cup of tea, Darkmella?" Belle was wiping every available surface with a cloth duster. "We've got low-fat milk."

Lachlan shook his head behind her.

"Eh… No thanks. Sorry, I didn't catch your name."

"Mrs. Maclennan." She began fetching cups from the cupboard. "Some coffee, then? Lachie, would you like coffee?"

"Nah. I'm all right."

"I've got some nice biscuits. Abernethy. Would you like a biscuit?"

"I'm OK, honest."

"An Abernethy, Darkmella? Would you care for one?"

"I like Abernethy," Alasdair piped up.

"Aye, I know *you* do." A half-open pack was plonked unceremoniously in front of him. "Some tea then, Lachie?"

"No, thank you."

"Well... it's there if you want it. And we've got orange juice in the fridge. The kind you like."

"I like all kinds of orange juice," Lachlan sighed.

"There's Branston Pickle too, if you fancy a sandwich. You as well, Darkmella. And cheddar. Nice cold meat."

"I'm fine, thanks."

"Take a seat then." Alasdair motioned to them. "Dinnae stand aroond cluttering the place."

"Well, they're there if you want tae have some," Belle pursed her lips. "There's rolls, as well, if you'd like a roll. In the bottom cupboard."

"You want a roll in the bottom cupboard, Dark?" Lachlan kept a straight face.

"I'm not hungry, Mrs. Watson," Dark lied. "We ate on the way."

"Well, there's Forfar Bridies for tea. Unless you'd like stovies." Her face registered sudden horror. "You're no a vegetarian, are you?"

"I am," Lachlan reminded her.

"I'm not," Dark smiled. "Except, I eat like a horse."

Lachlan's aunt and uncle stared at her blankly.

"I can make something else if you like. Lachie?"

"You no gonnae ask me?" Alasdair interjected.

"What do you want, then?" his wife snapped.

"I'll hae coffee, dear. And a digestive biscuit."

"Och, you're a nuisance, you are." The woman rummaged in the cupboard. "Would either of *you* pair like a digestive?"

Dark shook her head but Lachlan smiled impishly.

"Have you got any Custard Creams?"

"Oh, no, Lachie, I havnae." The woman seemed genuinely distressed. "I never thought tae get them in."

A frown creased her already furrowed brow.

"I thought you didnae like Custard Creams?"

"Cannae stand them. Just wondered if you had any."

"Och, Lachie." She gave a nervous laugh. "I've got Dundee Cake. Darkmella, do you like Dundee Cake?"

"What's a Dundee Cake?" Dark shot Lachlan a questioning look.

"I love Custard Creams," Alasdair peered over the top of his newspaper. "She never offers tae get me bloody Custard Creams."

"You dinnae deserve Custard Creams." Belle started making coffee. She seemed cursed with an inability to stay still.

"*I* dinnae deserve Custard Creams? What's the bloody laddie done tae deserve them?"

"He's a guest." Belle pointed proudly at the shell-shocked pair. "Eh, dear? Two guests."

"Well, awa and get me my bloody digestives, then."

"Alasdair!" his wife cried angrily. "Will you stop swearing?"

"I said biddy, not bloody. Biddy digestives."

"Could you no go oot and... dae something in the garden?"

"Awa you! Can I no get tae speak tae Darkmella?" The fact that he hadn't tried to engage Dark in a conversation of any type seemed to have escaped him. "The laddie hardly ever comes over, anyway."

He fastened Lachlan with a steely stare.

"Could you no visit your aunt a bit mair often?"

"I've been in Europe," Lachlan reminded him. "At the Venice Biennale?"

"He's busy, you old grump! I forgot you were coming, Lachie. Otherwise, I'd have got some things in and tidied up a bit."

She gave an ashamed laugh.

"I just cannae seem tae be bothered these days. I used to keep the place nice." She placed three coffees on the table, ignoring Lachlan and Dark's protests. "Help yourself tae milk and sugar."

"Dinnae worry about it, Aunty," Lachlan gave up and poured milk into his cup. "It's just a flying visit."

"Aye." Alasdair went back to reading. "It's always just a bloody flying visit."

"Alasdair! Will you behave?"

"I am bloody behaving! Will you calm down?"

"We tried tae call and say we were on our way." Lachlan began.

"The phone's no working," Alasdair jerked a calloused thumb at an ancient landline fastened to the wall.

"The wee dog bit through the cable," Belle explained. "We're thinking of getting rid of it."

"What?" Dark gasped. Lachlan seemed unfazed.

"That so you can offer me its dog biscuits?"

"Eh?" His aunt shook her head before realisation dawned on her. "Och no, Lachie! We're no getting rid of the wee dog."

"Stupid boy," Alasdair grunted.

"Alasdair!" Belle punched his arm. "No, we're thinking of getting rid of the telephone. It's too much trouble."

"Too much trouble?" Dark glanced at Lachlan.

"Oh, aye." Belle swatted at a tiny Pomeranian, napping on one of the chairs. Dark hadn't even noticed it was there. "Sherry! Get doon aff the seat."

"Gie it a kick," her husband suggested.

"Alasdair! The wee dog knows when you're talking aboot it."

"How can a telephone be trouble?" Lachlan groaned.

"We dinnae need it. Nobody ever calls us."

"What if you have tae reach the doctor again?" Alasdair reprimanded.

"Och, I dinnae ken."

"She'll no call him, anyway. Bloody woman."

There was silence for a while, while they all sipped their drinks. Finally, Alasdair put his paper away.

"Do you like *The Corries*, Darkmella?"

"No," Lachlan replied quickly. "She really, really doesn't."

"Och, awa you."

"I don't know," Dark said cautiously. "What's a Corrie?"

"Belle. Where's *The Corries* CD?"

"Darkmella's maybe not wanting tae listen to *The Corries*, Alasdair," his wife warned.

"How the hell would you know? Do you read Rabbie Burns, Darkmella?"

Lachlan's expression shifted from resignation to outright dismay.

"Belle... where's the Rabbie Burn's book? A great poet. Better than aw that American rubbish. What is it? Bob Dylan? Better than Bob Dylan."

"Alasdair! Will you behave?"

"I'll get the bloody book myself." The man stood up, stomach wobbling.

"It'll be in the presser upstairs, beside the photo albums." Belle turned to Dark. "We've got the sweetest pictures of Lachie. He was a bonny wee laddie."

"Shame how he turned oot." With that parting shot, Alasdair left the room.

"Alasdair!" Belle shouted after him. "He's a bonnie big laddie noo, as well. But bring doon the photo albums, so his girlfriend can see."

"She's not my girlfriend." Lachlan lowered his head onto the table and Dark sniggered. One pleading eye looked up at her as he mouthed the word *help*.

"I would love to stay and look at them, Mrs. Watson." Dark tapped her mobile. "But I have an interview to do in about 20 minutes. I'm so sorry."

"Well, you'll just have tae come back another time." The woman said brightly. "I'll get in Custard Creams."

She saw them to the door, then went upstairs to berate her husband some more.

Dark couldn't stop laughing.

"Holy shit, *Lachie*," she managed between gasps. "What are they like?"

"I think I need a Valium." Lachlan leaned weakly back on his car door. "And a bit of Dundee Cake."

"I can hardly stand," Dark guffawed again, wiping her eyes. "*Darkmella?* You are so mean!"

She rested her head against his chest and he put an arm around her. Dark glanced up, grinning, and their eyes met.

Neither looked away.

Lachlan reached out a hand towards her face, and Dark recoiled.

"It's all right." He wiped some crumbs off her cheek. "You cannae go to an interview looking like you raided the cookie jar."

Dark flinched again. Inwardly, this time.

"I lied about that to save you."

"Then meet me back at my place and we'll have proper coffee." He gave an impish grin. "Did you think I was going tae try and kiss you just then?"

"No!" she blushed. "Well, maybe. Yes. I'm sorry."

She reddened even more.

"It was presumptuous of me. But y'know, I'm still getting over…"

"I understand entirely." Lachlan opened his car door. "But I do like you, Dark Arrowsmith."

"Everyone does." She recovered her composure, got into her vehicle and drove off, still mentally berating herself.

As soon as she was out of sight, Aunt Belle came hobbling back.

"What were you thinking bringing that woman here?" she hissed. "She's a fucking reporter!"

"She insisted and, besides, she's only a features writer. It's not the same thing." He put an arm round her shoulder. "Dinnae worry, I'm keeping an eye on her just in case."

"Are you, though?" The old woman shrugged him off and pointed to a dirt track leading east. "Look. She's taken the long way round. She'll go right past the barns."

"So what, Auntie?" Lachlan tried to sound reassuring. "This is rural land and they're empty. The Laird is gone. The past is the past."

"The past is a sleeping dog that'll wake up and bite if you poke it," She slapped his broad chest. "You, of all people, should know that."

"You're right." Lachlan hung his head. "I'm sorry."

"Then keep an eye on her and make sure *you're* the only one doing the poking."

"Auntie!" He threw up his hands. "That is *so* inappropriate."

It took Dark ten minutes to traverse the circular dirt road until she reached the B45 again. When she finally drew up at Lachlan's house, he was sitting on the doorstep with two steaming mugs.

"No sugar or milk," he said. "Just the way you like it."

"What makes you think that?

"You're called Dark and you dress like a vampire. Despite that, you seem sweet enough."

"Christ," Dark groaned. "Which middle-aged dad calendar did you nick *that* joke from."

"Ooooh. Burned." Lachlan blew on his fingers. "I'll have tae up my game."

He indicated the kitchen.

"There's milk and sugar on the table."

"As a matter of fact, you're right." Dark accepted the mug. "I take it black."

They sat and stared at the scenery for a while.

"So… Aftonhouse," Dark said, finally. "Its own little world, as far as I can see."

"I wouldnae disagree with that."

"Elspeth and Frankie Cameron think it's boring."

"Yet they're still here," Lachlan shrugged. "Mind you, the village was bigger at one time. Then the council built a highway that went right past Aftonhouse rather than through it. Pretty much a death knell for the place."

He looked at her sadly.

"Even my best mate, Billy Milne, left. Been gone a year now and I haven't heard from him once."

"Oh." Dark sipped her coffee. "You've no idea why he left?"

"Not a clue."

Dark let it go. But, as a confidence trickster, she'd developed a keen sense for bullshit.

Lachlan was hiding something.

Aftonhouse Pub 2024

Dark and Elspeth

When she got back to the cottage, Dark flopped on the bed, got out her mobile and dialled.

Cameron's grocery store, a female voice answered.

"Is that you, Elspeth? It's Dark Arrowsmith here. The journalist?"

Oh, I'm sorry. Mum's not around, I'm afraid.

"Actually, it's you I wanted to talk to."

Really? The voice sounded surprised.

"You said you found Aftonhouse a bit dull." Dark kicked off her boots. "And I don't know anyone here, so I wondered if you'd fancy a girl's night out?"

She mentally crossed her fingers.

"Just say no if you don't want to. I realise I'm pretty much a stranger and you might be busy."

Are you kidding? I'll take any excuse to go for a drink. A stranger's just a friend you haven't made yet. Unless they're a serial killer, of course.

Dark smiled.

She found Elspeth seated in a booth in the hotel bar, sipping vodka and Coke. The pub was more basic than the restaurant but there was just as much tartan. Elspeth was wearing jeans and a t-shirt under a brightly patterned waistcoat. With makeup on and bright red hair cascading down to her shoulders, she was quite a looker.

Dark ordered wine and slid into the seat opposite.

"Right," she said. "I don't like whisky. I used to have a dog called Brain Haemorrhage. I've always worn boots, even to the beach, not the done thing in Australia. When I was born, I was covered in hair but it all fell off and, as a teenager, I had my own business cleaning out people's bins. They get very smelly in the heat of Queensland."

Elspeth looked confused.

"I'm introducing myself," Dark explained.

"The boots are a sign you're afraid of intimacy," Elspeth replied. "Always ready to run or fight."

"Oh." Dark raised an eyebrow. "People usually ask about the dog."

"I presume it was dumb. A Dalmatian, perhaps."

"King Charles Spaniel," Dark grinned. "OK. I like you."

"Elspeth Cameron." The girl raised her glass. "I have a crush on the actor Mark Duplass, even though he's ugly as sin. I get drunk pretty easily, so be warned. My mum's my best friend cause I was the peculiar one at school and that opinion of me didn't change when I grew up. I once ran the mile in just under four minutes and my most prized possession is an ET lamp signed by Steven Spielberg."

"It seems we have nothing in common. Let's get drunk."

They burst out laughing.

The ice was broken. And it turned out they had plenty in common. A quick mind, sardonic turn of phrase and a shared sense of loneliness covered up with jokes and banter.

After an hour, both were feeling extraordinarily merry and relishing each other's company.

Dark felt it was time to make her move.

"I met Lachlan Robertson," she said. "We went out to dinner and I've been round to his place a couple of times."

"You're a smooth operator, right enough," Elspeth whistled. "Any romance on the cards?"

"I'm not looking for anything like that but I'll admit, he is quite charming." A thought struck Dark. "You and he weren't…"

"It was his best mate, Bill, I liked," the girl laughed. "Me and Billy Milne had an on-off relationship. More off than on but there wasn't anyone else around who came close to matching him."

She gave a sly smirk.

"Enough of my failed romances. I take it you want to know all about Lachie?"

"That obvious, huh?" Dark blushed. "Though I wouldn't mind hearing about Billy too."

"You can't really talk about one without the other and, to be honest, it's quite a story." Elspeth stood up. "I'll get us a couple of drinks, then set the scene."

When she came back, she put down the glasses and looked around to make sure nobody was listening. She needn't have worried. Apart from a couple of men playing darts and a trio of old codgers clutching beers at the bar, the place was deserted. The barman was on his mobile playing some game. All the same, Elspeth kept her voice low.

"This has to be… How do you say it? Off the record?"

"I promise." Dark crossed her heart. "We're just chatting."

"Aftonhouse is remote and no tourist trap but it's very close to the coast." Elspeth leaned forwards. "There's money to be made in a place like that."

"I'm not sure what you mean."

"Billy's dad was a character named Big Don Milne. Everyone called him the Laird because he had a huge house to the east with a bunch of sheds. Claimed he ran a haulage operation and I suppose he did, in a way."

"What did he haul?" Dark was quick to realise what her companion was getting at.

"Beats me." The woman shrugged. "Drugs? Cigarettes? Whatever he was up to, it was illegal. I suppose 'smuggler' would be a polite term."

"Did the people here know?"

"It was an open secret but nobody was going to cross the Laird. He was a tough character and had the local police in his pocket. We left him alone and he left us alone. All the same, I had to keep my assignations with Bill quiet or nobody would have talked to me at all."

"What does this have to do with Lachlan?" Dark asked. "You said their stories were intertwined."

Bill was a quiet kid, much nicer than his father but always seeking his approval. He and Lachlan were devoted to each other from the day they met. They used to do jobs for Big Don which weren't... well... above board. Lachie got out of that life, though it always puzzled Bill how he managed it. But people here still keep him at arm's length and that's fine by him."

She looked around again.

"You really can't print any of this. It's not something we locals talk about."

"I honestly won't," Dark assured her. "Unless they discovered an abandoned gold mine together, it isn't the kind of story my editor wants. He's only looking for a puff piece."

"I trust you," Elspeth sounded relieved. "Anyway, Big Don had a bit of a love/hate relationship with his son. He was getting on but seemed reluctant to give Billy any responsibility. Treated him more like a lackey than an heir.

Bill told me he was secretly relieved but was still hurt by what he saw as a rejection."

Elspeth leaned over further until her face was inches from Dark's.

"Anyway, rumour has it some big deal came Don's way, about a year ago. I don't know the details but he sent Billy rather than one of his regular henchmen."

She stirred her drink with a swizzle stick, unsure of how to continue.

"Nobody ever saw Bill again. A couple of nights later, Don's men found Billy's truck hidden in the undergrowth of Spiral Wood. There was a spade in the back covered in dirt."

"I'm rapidly changing my opinion about this being a boring place," Dark breathed.

"You don't know the half of it." Elspeth glanced around a final time to make sure no one was paying attention. "Billy wasn't the only one who vanished. Big Don had a foreign cleaning woman. I forget her name but she disappeared too. So did all the illegal cash he kept in a huge safe."

The woman's cheeks were flushed. It was apparent she had wanted to share this story for some time, and alcohol had loosened her tongue.

"Local gossips tried to link the events, y'know? Billy and the cleaner left together after stealing Don's money. Lachie and the cleaner left together for Europe. Lachhie killed them both and stole Don's money. Pick your combination and someone here will have suggested it."

"And what's your take on it?"

I think it was pretty obvious." Elspeth finished her drink. "Billy was the one who stole his dad's money, then he buggered off. He had plenty of shady contacts, thanks to

Don. Would have been easy for him to buy another identity with his newfound wealth."

"Lachlan said he lost touch with Billy Milne a year ago but didn't elaborate."

"Lachie went off to Europe pretty frequently. I guess he could have taken the cleaner. She was a pretty little thing." She shrugged. "Whatever the truth, Big Don seemed convinced someone had done away with Billy and hid the body in Spiral Wood. Had his men search it more than once but it was an impossible task."

"Lachlan's back now," Dark said. "Didn't this Laird ask him about it?"

"Big Don was found dead not long after Bill disappeared. Suicide was the official verdict. I suppose he loved Billy more than anyone realised."

"You think it's possible Lachlan was involved in Billy's disappearance?" Dark wrinkled her nose. "I don't want to be hanging around with a killer, serial or otherwise."

"You have to be joking!" Elspeth shook her head. "Lachie is tough, unflappable and scared of nothing but he wouldn't harm a fly. Shave his head and you'd think he was a Buddhist monk."

She lowered her voice even more.

"Besides, Bill is alive."

"How do you know?"

"I got one typed note from him, mailed a few days after he vanished."

Dark's eyes widened.

"It said I was the only thing he regretted about leaving but he had no choice," Elspeth continued. "That he couldn't let me know where he was or where he had gone, for my own protection. Asked me not to tell Don, keep the letter to myself and promise to never reveal we had been together."

"But you're telling me?"

"It's been more than a year since I heard from Bill. He had his chance." She stirred her drink miserably. "It haunts me that I never told Don his son was all right. But I stuck to my word and it's too late now."

"Think Bill will ever resurface?"

"I live in hope." Elspeth gave a bark of laughter. "I bet he's living it large in Costa Rico or something, though, and good luck to him."

She glanced at her empty glass.

"Wish I was with him."

"I'll get another round." Dark took the hint and got out her purse. "You wouldn't… eh… happen to have a picture of Billy Milne?"

"The Laird would never allow it," Elspeth grunted. "If you're running illegal operations, you tend to keep a low profile for yourself and your family. Billy had no social media presence, was excluded from school photos and nobody here would have dared take a sneaky snap of him."

"I knew someone like that." Dark tried again. "But you two were lovers. You must have at least one selfie together?"

"The letter begged me to delete them, so I did. At the time, I presumed he had a good reason."

"That's more trust than I placed in my ex," Dark said.

"If anyone knows where Billy is, it should be Lachie," Elspeth mused. "The two of them were thick as thieves, excuse the pun. But he really doesn't seem to."

She thought for a moment.

"I can't give you more info on Lachie than that. He's a bit of a closed book, to be honest. Never socialises and rarely comes into the village. He's a sculptor or painter or something but I presume he already told you."

Dark nodded.

"That's more than most people here know, though they gossip about how he has enough money to avoid 'proper' work and travel so much."

"Maybe it's a cover and he's still a smuggler." As soon as the words were out of Dark's mouth, she realised how plausible an explanation it was.

"Oh." Elspeth bit her lip. "I hope not. I hadn't thought of that."

"I'll get that round." Dark walked over and ordered more alcohol at the bar. She tapped her lip with a long, painted nail while it was poured.

"Lachlan Robertson," she muttered. "What a dark horse you're turning out to be."

Half an hour later, the closing bell rang. Elspeth waited outside with Dark until the taxi arrived.

"Why do you stay here?" Dark asked. "You seem too lively for this little place."

"I've thought about it." She looked around. "But one bar is much the same as another and a mountain is as impressive as any skyscraper."

"No hankering to get out into the big bad world?"

"There's a lot to recommend about sitting back and letting the big, bad world get on with its business. I've got Instagram and YouTube."

"Of course." Dark wrinkled her nose. "I must be getting old."

But she suspected the real reason Elspeth stayed was that she was waiting in case Billy Milne ever returned.

"Proper company is better, though." Elspeth kissed her cheek. "Let's do this again."

"Absolutely," Dark agreed. "Here's my cab."

She held up one finger.

"By the way, have you ever heard of a man called Martin Cindrić?"

"No. But he sounds very exotic." Elspeth tottered up the street towards her house, waving as she went. "Thanks for a lovely night!"

Dark sat in the back of the cab, feeling tipsy. Elspeth had shared her deepest secrets with a total outsider and she was jealous of that openness. Dark had been abandoned, too. Who could *she* confide in?

She got out her phone and texted Lewis. One sentence.

I know who Spiral Wood is, Lew.

Her finger hovered over the *send* button.

No. Not yet. She still had too many questions and needed to find the answers herself. She deleted the message and typed another.

Hope you are good, Lew. I haven't found Spiral yet but the scenery is nice.

He didn't reply.

-Part III-

If he listens to music, it's the sound of running water
If he falls, it's down a slope of turf into the bushes
If he recites, it's from the Beast Epic of Alexandria
If he is seduced, it's a river of electricity
If he is curious, he attempts to draw
If he calls, it's about weather patterns
If he sings, it's 'Tyger, Tyger'
and if he escapes, he's swift of foot.
Camille Guthrie. *My Boyfriend*

The Road to Merchiston Point 2023

Lachlan and Billy

The big white truck had left any shred of civilization behind. Now Billy and Lachlan were on a dirt track winding its way between low hills towards the coast. Gulls screeched overhead, the north wind buffeting them around the sky.

"I still dinnae understand," Lachlan was saying. "You've never gotten much respect from your father, and this is not the life you wanted, yet you're still here."

"You never give up, eh?" Billy groaned. "As I said earlier, you don't say no to Big Don and you *don't* piss him off."

He glanced around.

"You remember our neighbour Gordon Crabbe's rottweiler? The one I called Total Bastard."

"Not really."

"Sure you do," Bill cajoled. "He spent his entire life lolling over Crabbe's eight-foot fence and I never saw his bottom half. This led me to one of two conclusions. Either he had the rear legs of a giraffe, or he was on stilts."

"Maybe he was standing on his kennel."

"Too far-fetched. Anyway, he'd go into a slavering frenzy every time he saw me, hence the dog's name. He probably trained it that way cause he hated my dad so much."

"Does this story hae a point?"

"Yeah. One day, Don was ranting and raving about Crabbe. I don't know what he did but dad was furious. Shouting that he was going to kill him and his fucking dog. Next day Total Bastard was gone. Don denied having anything to do with his disappearance but I'm not dumb. Crabbe loved that pooch."

"Maybe he was protecting you from it," Lachlan countered. "He loves you in his own weird way. Anyway, what's he going tae do if you say goodbye? Disappear you as well?"

"Course not. Problem is, I don't have any money of my own. Don says everything will get left to me once he's dead but I don't want to wait *that* long."

"Maybe he thinks you should make your own way in the world. In which case, he's got a point. You're smart enough."

"Easy for you to say." Billy punched his friend's arm. "You're a regular Michelangelo."

"I made another big sale last month." Lachlan tried not to sound smug. "Though I trust you'll keep that tae yourself."

"Way to go!" Billy threw an arm round his shoulder. "I'm proud of you."

"Eyes on the road, Bill. I'd like tae live long enough tae flog another."

"You're right, though," Billy swerved to avoid a startled rabbit. "I'm thinking this might be my last job."

"Really?

"I don't mind ferrying illegal cigarettes or bales of cannabis," Billy said. "If folk want to buy that shit, it's their lookout. But this trip has made the Laird nervous and if he's moving into more serious stuff, I refuse to be part of it."

"What will you do?"

"I've always fancied living in Edinburgh. It's not too big but nice and cosmopolitan."

He pulled a face.

"Course, I'd have to think of some way to make money without having to get an actual job."

"That's the spirit." Lachlan patted his shoulder. "I'm proud of you too."

Glasgow 2024

Dark, Spiral and Lewis

Dark and Lewis sat in Glasgow's Manatee Restaurant, eating lunch. Both were dressed in expensive clothes, blending in perfectly with the plush surroundings. Lewis wore a grey tailored suit and silk tie, while Dark had on a Chanel dress and carried a Salvatore Ferragamo bag.

"How's the romance going?" Lewis whispered. "Spiral seems head over heels."

"Pretty well," Dark replied. "Except for one small thing."

"There's probably some kind of pump for that on the internet."

"Idiot," she laughed. "No. We talk about all sorts of things but never his past. No matter how much I push, he just won't go into it. Says it's something he'd rather forget."

"And that's not good enough for you?"

"I love him. I want to know." She spooned risotto into her mouth. "What's the story, Lew? You're his best friend."

She thought for a moment.

"In fact, you seem to be his only friend."

"I'd tell you if I could but he's never opened up to me either."

"Oh. I got the impression you'd known each other forever."

"Nope. Only met him a few months ago." Lewis shook his head. "He had some shady connections and a mutual acquaintance put us in touch to pull a con together. He was a natural and we hit it off."

He looked at her openly.

"I trust him. If he doesn't want to dig up the past, I'm happy to let sleeping dogs lie."

"If I'm sleeping with this particular dog, I need a bit more than that."

"He could have made up a bunch of stuff, as any good trickster should." Lewis shrugged. "Instead, he's been honest and refused to tell you. That must count for something."

"There's the twisted logic of a con man on display," Dark snorted. "I didn't even believe his real name was Spiral Wood until he showed me his passport."

Her laugh turned into a groan.

"Although, it's almost certainly fake. Is he a…"

The door opened and Spiral entered. He wore a shabby coat with holes in it and his hair was unwashed. Under one arm he carried a battered violin. Ignoring them, he sat in the next booth and ordered the cheapest entrée on the menu. The waiter looked at him with undisguised suspicion.

When the snack came, Spiral quickly finished it and looked like he was about to leave. Before he could get up, the owner bustled over with a bill.

"Here you are, sir." He placed it on the table and waited.

"Oh, aye." Spiral searched his pockets. "Damn. I forgot tae bring ma cash."

"A credit card will do nicely." The owner didn't move. He had slicked-back hair and a comedy moustache that made him look like a pantomime villain.

"I dinnae have one." Spiral looked embarrassed. "Tell ye what, though. I've a mate outside who'll lend me the money."

He placed his violin on the table.

"This has got tae be worth a few quid. I'll leave it here while I go hit him up. He's just aroon the corner."

The owner raised an eyebrow.

"It's how I make mah livin man, know? Playing in the subway. Plus, I got it fae mah dad." Spiral looked apologetic. "So, I'll definitely come back, honest."

"On you go then. But be quick" The man folded his arms and Spiral shuffled out of the door. Dark and Lewis watched him leave, then turned to the owner and rolled their eyes.

"Sorry about that." The man was about to pick up the instrument when Dark grabbed his arm.

"Wait a moment." She had altered her accent to sound vaguely French. "May I see that violin, please?"

"Sure." The man handed it over. "Looks like it fell off the back of a lorry."

Dark's eyes widened.

"Sainte Mère du Christ," she breathed. "This is a Vieuxtemps Guarneri."

"Let me see." Lewis snatched it from her and studied the front. "It's inscribed with the name, sure enough, but any forger could have done that."

"He did not look like a forger. Good or otherwise."

Lewis hefted the instrument in one hand and studied the grain carefully.

"Oh my God, it's genuine," he gulped. "What has that bastard done to it? The thing's all scratched."

Dark took it back and ran her hand over the surface. She examined the fretwork, then put the body against her chin and plucked a few notes. A dumbfounded grin spread across her face.

"It is real," she announced. "There can be absolutely no doubt."

"What are you both talking about?" The restaurant owner frowned. "It looks like that guy used it to dig up the road."

Dark fished in her pocket and handed him a card.

Veronica Pascalle
ANTIQUARIES' DROUOT - Paris, France.

"This is a Vieuxtemps Guarneri violin," she said. "It does not matter what condition it is in. The body is solid. It is worth a fortune."

"Hah." The owner laughed. "How much exactly?"

"In this state? Two million euros."

"I'd say three million," Lewis argued. "More if it's properly restored."

The moustache quivered.

"Keep the instrument until we come back." Dark pulled a wad of notes from her bag and dumped them on the table. There had to be £300 in the pile.

"That should cover the bill and whatever the shabby gentleman ate, n'est pa?" She and Lewis struggled out of the booth. "We must find him right now."

"We're going to make that lucky bastard *exceedingly* rich." Lewis ran out of the door, Dark in tow.

The owner stared at the violin, unsure of what to do. Then he picked it up, headed into the back and emptied his safe.

As he returned, Spiral entered, clutching a ten-pound note.

"Sorry aboot that, mate," he said sheepishly. "Got your money, though."

The owner thought for a moment.

"It's me who should be sorry," he relented. "Treating someone who's obviously down on their luck so badly."

"Aw, it's fine. You got a business tae run."

"No. My daughter wants to learn the violin, so I'll do you a favour." He hugged the instrument. "I'll buy this off you."

"I told ye, man." Spiral shook his head. "It's the only way I have tae make money."

The owner looked at the door. The antique dealers might be back at any moment.

"I'll give you three grand in cash," he said. "Enough to buy yourself a brand-new violin with plenty left over."

"Why would you do that fur me?" Spiral's eyes narrowed.

"I used to be on the streets myself, at one time, playing the guitar," the owner lied. "You've pricked my conscience. I make plenty now and I want to pay something back."

"But it belonged to my dad. It's the only thing he left me when he died. It's been in mah family forever."

The owner glanced at the door again. Those posh bastards might return any second.

"I'll make it £5,000. That's all I have on the premises."

Spiral licked his lips hungrily.

"Sorry, Sammy. I cannae turn that kind of money doon, eh?"

"Sammy?"

"It's the name of mah violin."

"Of course it is." The owner grunted and handed over his cash. "I'm sure your da would understand."

Spiral pocketed his prize and nodded sadly.

"Please take good care of him. I'll buy Sammy back once I'm on mah feet again."

"I doubt that." The owner shooed him away. "Now, fuck off."

Moments later, Spiral left the restaurant with the £5000, leaving behind a useless violin he had purchased at a car boot sale.

Dark drove home with Lewis in the passenger side, both chatting animatedly. Spiral sat silently in the back, gazing moodily at the pylons and graffiti-daubed factories whizzing past.

"What's up, buddy?" Lewis turned in his seat. "I thought you'd be all smiles after that sweet manoeuvre."

Spiral was quiet for a while.

"I'm thinking this was my last con," he said eventually.

"What? *Why?*" Lewis's jaw dropped. "You could sell a man his own balls. Best grifter I ever saw."

"Problem is, I don't want to be seen," Spiral retorted. "Our faces are getting too well known and we have to keep going further and further afield."

"Yeah, but we're making a fortune." Lewis nudged Dark. "Can you talk some sense into him?"

"It's been fun, Lew. Best rush I ever had. Better than sex, even."

"Thanks for that," Spiral muttered.

"But I don't want to go to prison." Her hands tightened on the steering wheel. "I think Spiral's right. It's time to call it a day."

"What are you both going to do instead?" Lewis persisted. "Get jobs as parking attendants?"

"I want to settle down, partner," Spiral said. "We've all got plenty of money and… I'm in love."

"Aw, fuck." Lewis ran a hand through his curly hair. "You had to trot out the only line I'd sympathise with."

He patted Dark's knee.

"Told you he was the master of manipulation."

Once Dark had gone to bed, Lewis and Spiral sat in the living room, drinking and talking quietly.

"You're making a big mistake," Lewis warned. "We have an agenda and you need to stick to it."

"I will," Spiral objected. "A con this big needs time to set up. Get it wrong and we'll never be safe."

"You're stalling so you can spend more time with Dark."

"I love her, Lew."

"And she loves you. You're going to break her heart."

"When it's over, I'll come back."

"You won't be able to." Lewis took an angry swallow. "You *know* you won't. End it now."

"Don't you understand?" Spiral shot back. "She's my world. I never thought I could feel like that."

"You made a promise, buddy. And not just to me."

"I'll see things through to the bitter end. You know that much about me."

"I do," Lewis relented. "I also know it's not going to turn out the way you hope."

"Maybe not." Spiral finished his beer. "Yet, for once, I've *got* some hope."

He went to the fridge and fetched another couple of bottles.

"C'mon Lew. Be happy for me."

"I'll try." Lewis accepted the drink. "Just don't say I didn't warn you."

"That's the spirit," Spiral winked. "I'm going to come out on top this time. Then I'll marry her. You'll see."

Lewis stayed silent.

Lachlan's Barn 2024

Dark and Lachlan

"**C**an I come over?" Dark was up to her neck in bubbles, a washcloth wrapped around the phone.

Excuse me? Lachlan replied. *You're a wee bit muffled.*

"I'm in the bath," Dark explained. "I was asking if I could visit."

Only if you get dressed first. This is a respectable neighbourhood.

Dark now knew that wasn't strictly true but smiled anyway.

"I meant tonight. You promised to show me your sculptures."

Good job I dinnae do etchings, eh?

"Good job you don't do middle-aged dad jokes, eh? Oh. But you do."

Touché. She could tell he was grinning. *About 8.00 pm?*

"I'll be there."

She dried herself, wondering if he had been flirting with her again and how she felt about that. She didn't know the answer to either question.

"I always pick the mysterious ones," she muttered to herself.

Dark turned up on time. She was never late. Lachlan emerged from the house, wearing an expensive overcoat and carrying a flashlight.

"Time to test your knowledge of modern art." He offered her his arm. "Shall we?"

They made their way along the furrowed path towards the nearby aluminium barn. Lachlan produced a key, opened a padlock the size of his head and pulled off the chain fastening the double doors.

"What do you make your sculptures out of?" Dark sniggered. "Solid gold?"

"The police around these parts are not exactly reliable and I got a lot of nickable equipment." Lachlan slid open the doors and switched on the overhead lights.

Dark gaped.

The barn was huge, the cavernous inside cleared of all usual farm implements. The concrete floor was cleanly swept and one end held what looked like welding equipment and bags of plaster.

In the middle was an enormous cage. Lying inside was a fiberglass female nude. The face was devoid of features, so all the emotion in the piece had to be conveyed by her posture. The body was twisted in a way that suggested both ecstasy and agony. One hand was between her legs, either protecting herself or reaching orgasm. The other clutched the bars, knuckles white. Dark couldn't decide if she was being aroused or tortured. Either way, the sculpture emanated raw, primal power. So much that it was frightening.

"Holy fucking shit," she breathed.

"You dinnae like it?" Lachlan glanced sideways at her.

"It's exquisite." Dark couldn't tear her eyes away. "Truly stunning."

She shuffled nervously over to the object, as if it might spring to life at any moment.

"Can I touch it?"

"Knock yourself oot." Lachlan shrugged. "At the moment, it's called *Untitled Nude*, cause I cannae think of an appropriately pretentious title. It'll come."

Dark walked around the cage, studying the figure from every angle. At the bottom was a small plaque.

W. H. Art.

She gasped out loud.

"I've seen your work before!" she said. "A sculpture in Edinburgh's National Gallery. My ex said it was his favourite piece."

"Oh," Lachlan replied non-committedly. "That's probably just a coincidence."

"Quit the innocent act. The artist was listed as W.H. Art but there were no other details." Dark stared at him in astonishment. "That's *you*."

"I do everything through a dealer because I like my anonymity," Lachlan said evenly. "The villagers think I'm a struggling nobody, so it's my way of showing I trust you."

"My editor would go nuts over this." Dark arched an eyebrow. "And you don't really know me."

"I'm hardly Banksy, though it's a nice wee earner."

"It's got pride of place in the National bloody Gallery! Your stuff is famous."

"Trends change and, anyway, this one isnae for sale." Lachlan picked at the button on his coat. "Let's just say I'm hoping you'll decide tae treat me as your friend rather than a story."

"Hmmm. You got wine at your house?"

"I live alone in the arse end of nowhere." Lachlan grinned. "Got enough booze tae drown a hippo."

"Lead on then, friend. I get the feeling I only scratched your surface at the restaurant."

"Me too. You gave virtually nothing away about yourself and I'd like tae ken more."

"Can't promise." Dark waited until he had shut and padlocked the door. "You're not the only one with secrets."

This time, she offered him her arm.

"I'll do my best, though."

National Gallery, Edinburgh 2023

Dark and Spiral

Spiral and Dark wandered, hand in hand, round the National Gallery of Art on Edinburgh's Mound.

"I can't believe you dragged me in here when the sun is shining," Spiral moaned. "Don't you know how rare that is?"

"I want to get a bit of culture," Dark said.

"I guess that makes sense. You being from Australia and all."

"What's that supposed to mean, mate?" She squinted at him. "You saying we lack finesse."

"You lot think sticking a straw in a tin of Fosters is sophisticated."

"Cheeky!" Dark slapped his arm. "Mind you, some of the art in here was painted before the first white man set foot in Oz. This is my chance to see it in person."

"I'm rather fond of the giant renaissance tableaux myself." Spiral led her into a room lined with enormous biblical and mythological scenes in thick, ornate frames. "They often have a hidden element that only the perceptive observer can spot."

"Like the *Da Vinci Code*?" Dark was genuinely enthused by the prospect of a proper discussion.

"Totally. They all contain one figure who seems genuinely surprised to be there." Spiral pointed. "In that one, it's a cherub. In this, it's a camel. Look at his astonished expression."

"I might have known you wouldn't take it seriously," Dark scolded. "Don't know why. You're a pretty good artist yourself."

"I'm a good con artist." He brushed off the compliment. "Mind you, good art is often a con - or sleight of hand, at least."

He pointed to a huge scene.

"Check out that one. It's *The Vale of Dedham*, painted by John Constable in 1828."

Dark was impressed. The information plaque was too far off for Spiral to have read it.

"What's on the pastureland in the background?" he asked.

"Brown and white cows."

"You sure? Go right up take another look."

Dark did so. The 'cows' were simply small blobs of paint. No head, legs or tail to distinguish them as animals of any sort. Yet, from a distance, there was no question about what they were.

"Oh, wow!" She turned back. "That's amazing."

"I'm not in his league," Spiral said modestly. "Or, perhaps, nothing is quite what it seems when you look closely enough."

"See? Being here is making you go all profound."

"You're right. I'm off to the gift shop." He kissed her cheek. "Maybe I can get an umbrella with little Van Gogh sunflowers on it. It'll probably be raining again by the time we leave."

Dark wandered round on her own, marvelling at the treasures on display. *Woman Drying Herself* by Degas. *Olive Trees* by Vincent Van Gogh. *Haystacks* by Monet. *Lady Agnew Of Lochnaw* by John Singer Sargent. Raphael's *Bridgewater Madonna*. Da Vinci's *The Madonna Of The*

Yarnwinder. An Old Woman Cooking Eggs by Diego Velázquez, Rembrandt's *A Woman In Bed.* Botticelli's *The Virgin Adoring The Sleeping Christ Child.*

She looked at the date underneath. 1485.

"Holy fuck," she breathed, feeling slightly sacrilegious at the blasphemy.

Dark spent a good ten minutes admiring *Christ Blessing* by El Greco, moved to tears by its solemn beauty. She wished Spiral was there to share the moment. Perhaps he considered himself a distraction. Tearing herself away, she wandered into the next room.

Spiral was sitting on a velvet-covered bench, staring at a sculpture.

It resembled a colossal window set in the middle of the room. Sandwiched between the panes were two mobile phones with holes cut in the glass so you could touch them - while wires led down to chargers on the floor. In one corner was a large crack that seemed to threaten imminent destruction for the whole edifice.

"This is my favourite piece." He looked up. "*The Bride Stripped Bare by Her Suitors, Again.*"

"I've heard of that. Marcel Duchamp?" Dark frowned. "Only, they didn't have mobiles back then."

"That was *The Bride Stripped Bare by Her Suiters, Even,*" he corrected. "This is an homage, I guess you could say."

"I'm not much into modern art," Dark conceded. "I've no idea what this means."

"Go to the mobile on the left." Spiral got up and walked around the sculpture. "Look at me and press the camera button."

Dark did so. Spiral was bathed in a red glow and his face had been transformed into an evil sneer. Behind him, a shadowy wraith hovered ominously.

She jerked her head back. He was on the other side, completely normal. She looked through the viewfinder again. The alarming image was back.

"Pretty chilling. Some kind of app?"

"I presume so. If you look in the camera gallery there are hundreds of clips of ordinary people turned into fearsome, haunted caricatures."

Dark moved to the other mobile, checking if it did the same. It appeared to have slipped down from the hole in the glass and gotten wedged between the panes.

"It's just out of reach of my fingers," she said. "Should we tell someone?"

"It's always like that. What's more, the right one is permanently on full charge. The left one, however, has a flaw that means the battery empties quickly. When it goes dead, the charger briefly comes on and powers it up again."

"Why can't I touch it?"

"I presume that's the whole point. Most people reckon the artist is representing the fundamental lack of trust and communication in the modern age."

He scratched his chin thoughtfully.

"I'm betting there's more to it than that."

"Give me your pearls of wisdom, babe."

"I think there are pictures in the second camera the artist doesn't want anyone else to see. Something truly important, flickering briefly to life, hidden under the surface of a world obsessed with trivial sharing."

Dark read the inscription underneath.

"W.H. Art. That's obviously not his real name."

"Nobody knows his identity. But he's in galleries all over Europe."

"I prefer your stuff. You have real talent. I mean it."

"I'd rather write than draw."

"I've been meaning to ask about that." Dark pulled him down onto one of the velvet-covered benches. "I see you typing away, but you never show anything to me."

"It's dabbling, that's all. Mostly autobiographical nonsense." He shrugged. "I've tried to do serious stuff, but what's the point? It won't last."

"Don't say that. Look at what's hanging around you on the walls. These works are timeless."

"You know what all these lasting masterpieces have in common?" Spiral was serious this time. "They're made by true outsiders, simply observing a scene, then interpreting and describing it in paint. That's why they've lasted. They're dispassionate historical observations disguised as beauty."

"I'm not sure what you're getting at."

"When most people paint or write, they bare their soul. But they mainly do it in the context of their time and culture and that makes the work archaic as soon as they've put down the brush or pen. Like slavers or colonials or misogynists, they unconsciously embody traits coming generations will find intolerable."

He heaved a sigh.

"Someday, the fact that characters in stories eat meat, ignore refugees, tolerate racism, repress women and allow religion to sway them will be the undoing of most authors and artists. They just beat on, boats against the current, borne back ceaselessly into the past."

He nodded morosely towards the sculpture.

"*That's* what W.H. Art is trying to say. That we engineer our own obsolescence. If the world improves, and I hope it will, each previous generation is sleepwalking its way to the wrong side of history. A true artist merely shows you what he sees and keeps the most personal stuff to himself."

Dark stared at him.

"You're deeper than you pretend, Spiral Wood." She took his hand. "Tell you what, let's go get a coffee and one of those nice umbrellas, eh?"

"Sure," he grinned. "This place has a decent café."

Robertson Farmhouse 2024

Dark and Lachlan

Dark and Lachlan relaxed in leather chairs Lachlan had pulled round so they faced each other. Dark's coat and boots were piled in a corner and she wore a sleeveless black top. Both held full glasses, and a bottle of wine in an ice bucket stood on the coffee table next to them. An already empty bottle lay on the floor.

"I should have checked how you're going tae get home." Lachlan sounded concerned. "You cannae drive after this."

"Have the local taxi driver on speed dial," Dark chuckled. "He says I'm the only person who calls him this time of year, so I've got it covered."

"We've also covered music, politics, literature, the best stuff on Netflix and, for some unfathomable reason, medieval art." Lachlan leaned back. "Laughed a lot. Agreed on most things."

He shrugged.

"Yet, we're like two swordfighters looking for an opening in the other's armour."

"While afraid to let down our own guard, eh?" Dark nodded. "What does the sculpture I saw mean?"

"Nice circumvention there. It's completely open tae interpretation."

"You really tour round art galleries in Europe?" Dark sounded envious. "I'd love to do that."

"I like to travel. There's a lot to see out there."

"I went for a drink with Elspeth Cameron," Dark said. "She was talking about you, Big Don Milne and his son Billy. You said he was your best mate."

"I did."

"She told me Billy disappearing so suddenly caused a bit of a stir. A mystery, even."

"The locals do love tae gossip," Lachlan said stiffly. "And that doesnae sound like the research you're meant to be doing."

"Keep your shaggy hair on," Dark reassured him. "We were just yakking. Anyway, Elspeth wasn't clear on any details, probably because she was pissed."

"Some things are painful to talk about." Lachlan downed his drink and poured another. "That's not just me being evasive. Billy *was* my closest friend but I've honestly no idea where he is. I wish I did."

This time, he seemed sincere.

"What was he like?" Dark asked.

"Charming. Handsome. Impulsive. A forceful sort, with everyone but his dad. They were… wary of each other. People assumed Bill was a bit of a thug and he was wild, nae doubt about that. But, deep down, he was a lost soul and a decent guy. Well-read and smart as a whip."

He thought for a moment.

"I'd tell you more but, even though I was his best mate, he was a bit of a closed book."

"That's what Elspeth said about you," Dark laughed. "Those exact words."

"That's Aftonhouse," Lachlan snorted. "A place of mystery, where people go to forget and be forgotten."

"I don't think we need to delve into each other's past right now," Dark apologised. "I'm happy to bask in your fine company."

"Good." Lachlan seemed mollified. "Most people annoy the hell out of me, yet there's something about you I'm drawn to…"

"It's the freckles, isn't it?"

"Absolutely."

"Want me to let my guard down?" She put a hand to her face and peeked at him through entwined fingers. "Truth is, I find you rather attractive."

There. She'd said it.

"I'll go one better." Lachlan raised his glass. "At the risk of sounding wanky and, accepting your present situation, I think you are absolutely beautiful."

"Wow." Dark fumbled in her pockets. "Can I push my luck by asking if I can go out on the balcony and have a cigarette?"

She pulled a face.

"It's a filthy habit, I know."

"I dinnae mind if you smoke in here," Spiral said. "It's cold out."

"Thank you, but I want to look at the forest. It's hypnotically eerie."

"I can roll a joint if you like."

"Seriously?"

"There is absolutely nowhere in the highlands you cannae buy drugs. There's nothing else tae do."

"You go ahead. I'll pass this time." Dark got up. "Weed tends to make me sleepy and I'm having fun."

While Lachlan rolled his joint, Dark stood on the balcony, peering into the gloom. A full moon floated in the black sky, turning the treetops to silver fractals. Damn! This forest was truly sinister.

Lachlan came out to join her.

"You haven't lit your cigarette."

"I'm trying to quit. Just holding it is better than nothing."

"It's freezing." Lachlan rubbed her bare arm. "Want me tae get you a jumper?"

Dark went rigid.

"I'm being overfamiliar." He quickly removed his hand. "I'm an idiot."

"It's not that." She pointed. "I just spotted someone down there."

"Where?" Lachlan peered into the blackness. "I dinnae see anything."

"Someone was hiding in the trees, I swear."

"I believe you, though I cannae imagine why anybody would be lurking in the woods at this time of night."

"There was a large man looking right up at me." Dark backed away from the rail. "I'm probably being paranoid but I could have sworn he was holding some kind of pistol."

"Hold on." He vanished inside. Seconds later, he was back, carrying a high-powered rifle with a telescopic sight.

"Any sign of our intruder?"

"What the fuck?" Dark stared at the gun. "Is that even legal?"

"My father taught me how tae shoot and, despite the fact I had nae interest in learning, I took tae it. That's life, I suppose."

"You don't...?" Dark tried to hide her disappointment.

"I have nae desire to hunt helpless animals, if that's what you're asking." Lachlan shook his head. "I'm a vegetarian, remember?"

"Oh, yeah."

"Only damned one in the highlands, as far as I can see. Know how hard it is to get tofu around here?" He rolled his eyes theatrically. "I was just being macho tae impress. I'm not kidding, though. Anyone out there must be up tae something dodgy and we're pretty isolated."

"Let's go in. He's obviously gone." Dark put the cigarette back in its packet. "This forest gives me the absolute heebs and sighting a potential prowler doesn't make it any more inviting."

They sat down again. Lachlan had found an ashtray and was lighting his joint.

"Are you sure nobody lives around here but you?" Dark asked nervously.

"Not a soul." Lachlan took a drag. "Look. If you're worried, why don't you stay the night?"

"Oh." Dark was taken aback. "I… eh…"

"In my spare room," Lachlan added quickly. "If anything ever happens between us, I dinnae want you to wake up regretting it because you'd been drinking."

"You think that's a possibility, eh?"

"I'm a glass is half full kind of guy," He held up his drink. "Literally."

He took another drag.

"Not tonight, though. You can ply me with wine but, freckles or not, I hae my self-respect tae consider."

Robertson Farmhouse 2024

Dark and Lachlan

Next morning, Dark showered, combed her hair and came downstairs wearing a fluffy white bathrobe she'd found in the bedroom cupboard. She had agonised briefly over whether to get dressed but her clothes were wrinkled after lying on the floor all night. Deciding to retain some modicum of decency, she had put on her boots. That ought to do it.

She needn't have worried. Lachlan was only wearing a pair of chino shorts, his broad torso silhouetted by sunshine flooding through the kitchen window. He was busy making coffee and there was a plate of toast on the table.

"Morning," he said, glancing over his shoulder. "Sleep well?"

"I wasn't asleep," Dark sat, took a piece of toast and bit into it. "Try unconscious. Feeling surprisingly refreshed, though."

"Here you go." Lachlan placed a mug in front of her and slid into the chair opposite. "That was a fun night."

"It was, from what I recall."

Dark weighed up her possibilities while he spread jam on his toast. They had shared a lot the previous evening. Nothing of any great importance, but she felt completely comfortable with him. She could go back to talking about trivialities or try to preserve that closeness.

"I was a bit surprised by you last night," she said.

"Was it because I played Thot Squad? I believe that OG be down with da kids right now, you feel?"

Dark almost spat out her drink.

"Ok." Lachlan kept a straight face. "What exactly did I do?"

"You told me I was beautiful, for starters."

"Could have been the drink talking. Only, I'm sober now and my opinion hasnae changed."

"Why didn't you try anything?"

"Told you. I was being a gentleman."

"Bollocks." Dark pulled a face. "I think I made it rather clear I fancied you."

"It was mentioned. But you were pissed as well."

"You snooze, you lose, mate." She finished her slice and looked hungrily at the plate.

"Help yourself tae more." He pushed the toast towards her.

"That's pretty much what I was hinting at last night." She pursed her lips. "I'm glad you didn't, though. Maybe you *are* a gentleman."

"Nah, it's not that." He looked thoughtful. "You want tae know the truth?"

"Of course."

"I grew up in Aftonhouse. A place men are supposed tae be strong and stoic. Where women are expected tae giggle at what we say and read soapy magazines."

"I did wonder if you had a copy of *Hello! Magazine* lying around for your female guests to peruse." Dark forgot for a moment she was supposed to be representing just such a publication. And that, according to Frankie, Lachlan never had guests.

"I watch the news. I read articles." He sat back in his seat. "And there's always some bloke bleating about how they dinnae ken their place in the world anymore. That everything is too PC. That *they* have an emotional burden as well."

He rolled his eyes.

"They complain that, aye, they're total feminists but the goalposts keep changing and they're no sure how they're meant tae *act*."

"And you'd rather be striding across the heather showing off your pecs, while the little woman waits at home?"

"I'm saying men aren't confused in the slightest." He peered at her over the rim of his cup. "They've had it good over the last few thousand years and they sure as shit dinnae want that tae change."

Dark raised an eyebrow.

"They ken women are easily their equals and probably their superiors," he continued. "That they should enjoy the same pay and opportunities and their views should command respect. What's more, men are happy tae accept that. With one big proviso."

"And that would be?"

"Can I go off at a tangent for a second?"

"Can't stop you, can I? I'm only a lowly female."

"You're Australian, right? You've tried tae make amends for the way you acted in the past. In your schools and assemblies, you pay homage tae the traditional land and its indigenous guardians. You're talking aboot changing the date of Australia Day because it actually celebrates the white invasion of a country beginning the annihilation of the Aborigines."

"We don't call them…"

"Aye. You dinnae call them Aborigines anymore because it's racially insensitive. Your government even officially apologised for the way they'd been treated."

"You're certainly up to date on world affairs." Dark sipped her coffee and wondered where he was going with this.

"But, obviously, you'll never give them the thing they really want. Their country back or even a proper say in how it's run."

"It's a bit more complicated than that…" Dark began.

"Men are exactly the same with women." Lachlan interrupted. "We apologise for the way you're treated. Make wee concessions. Say we understand. Yet, when you want real equality, we complain that it's mair complicated than that."

"Touché" Dark lifted her cup in salute.

"*Don't keep calling us out on every little thing*; we cry. *We're trying!*" He finished his coffee and got up to make some more. "No, we're not. If we were, you wouldnae have tae keep calling us out."

"You sound remarkably like…" Dark began. Then she stopped herself.

"Open-minded men? They may genuinely feel bad, but they're only willing tae jump through hoops if it's part of an act. If they can subtly stay in charge."

He chuckled briefly.

"So, I'm not a gentleman. I just dinnae like hypocrisy."

He began to spoon more granules into the cafetière, his back to her.

"If a woman wants tae have sex with me? She should say so, loud and clear. A drunken hint doesnae give me the right tae presume."

"How the fuck did you just manage to mansplain feminism to me?" Dark blinked rapidly. "Sound enlightened *and* condescending at the same time?"

"Dunno. I'm still trying tae find my place in the world. I'll be all right, though. After all, I dinnae identify as being Scottish, male or white."

"You almost sound serious."

"It's a handy way of not taking the blame for anything. I cannae believe more folk haven't cottoned on tae that."

The cafetière gave a burp. Dark stared at his naked back. To hell with caution.

She pushed her chair away and circled the table. As Lachlan turned, she grabbed a bread knife from the counter and held it to his throat, so forcefully it almost sank into the man's flesh. To her astonishment he did not show the slightest trace of fear.

"This is new." His eyes held hers. "I suppose one last cigarette is out of the question."

"I want you to fuck me right now," Dark whispered. "That equal enough for you?"

"No need tae threaten violence. I would have said yes anyway."

"Sorry." Dark's hand trembled. "I sometimes get carried away with a flair for the dramatic."

She dropped the blade and crushed her lips against his. Her robe fell open and he pushed it from her shoulders to the floor. Thrusting both hands into her hair, he pulled Dark's head back and kissed her neck and breasts as she blindly fumbled and pulled down his shorts.

Stepping out of them, Lachlan lost his balance and staggered forwards. Dark landed on the table, wrapping both legs around his waist. Toast and empty coffee mugs skittered across the wooden top.

"Are we having comedy sex?" he gasped.

"We're having every kind of sex." Dark pushed Lachlan back onto the wooden chair and straddled him.

They pawed and clawed, bit and kissed, moaning and swearing. At some point, they landed on the floor, and as Dark came, she actually screamed.

When they were finally spent, Lachlan held her head against his chest and stroked her cheek while she cried.

Later, they sat naked in the garden, drinking pear juice.

"You kept your boots on the whole time," Lachlan chuckled. "There's something incredibly erotic about that."

He smoothed down her hair.

"I have a pair of wellingtons I can wear if that's your thing. They've got wee turtles on them but it's all the Oban Co-Op had in stock."

He glanced at her.

"So, what happens now?"

"Are you asking if this is a one-night stand?" Dark said. "Or… eh… day stand?"

"I'd certainly like it tae be more."

"Me too. It's just that…"

"You're still in love with your boyfriend."

"I was thinking about what you said," Dark sighed. "I guess I should accept he's my ex-boyfriend, eh?"

"That's up tae you. I cannae feel guilty aboot it if he left you. I dinnae even know the guy's name and I'm fine keeping it that way."

"You're not curious?"

"I have a sort of rule. Actually, it's more like a cast iron rule," Lachlan chose his words carefully. "Let the past stay in the past. Aftonhouse is a place where people keep their business to themselves and that's how I like it."

Lachlan tilted his head back, letting the morning sun warm his face. Dark could see a thin red line on his throat.

"Anyway, you'll be going back tae Edinburgh soon," he added. "When you're done with your story."

"Let's not think about that now. I'm taking the day off."

"God. I have something tae show you, if you like."

"OK."

"Drive over to yours, get a change of clothes and I'll meet you shortly. Wear sensible footwear."

He looked down at Dark's Dr Martins.

"Aye. Those will do."

"Sounds good." She bit her lip. "Lachlan?"

"Yes?"

"When I put that knife to your throat, you didn't even baulk." Dark frowned. "Weren't you scared?"

"Highland men dinnae show fear, lassie." His voice went down an octave. "That's why we charge into battle wearing kilts and no undies."

He tilted his head quizzically.

"I am wondering why you did it, though."

"I figured it was stronger than a hint and I didn't want to be turned down twice. Bad for my fragile ego."

"As if I would." Lachlan leaned over and kissed her again. "I'll get dressed."

Once he was gone, Dark stared at the far off hills. Pulling cons, Spiral had been in awe of her ability to lie on the spot, so she had taken pride in it too.

Not anymore.

She knew exactly why she had threatened Lachlan. It was nothing to do with sex.

And she hated herself for it.

Edinburgh Zoo 2023

Dark and Spiral

After driving home, Dark put on a jumper and jeans. She glanced at Spiral's memento box and tried to ignore it. But Lachlan hadn't arrived yet.

She opened the lid and removed a small pad. On the front, in black pen, was written.

Spiral's Notebook. Get it?

"Let's have a holiday."

Dark and Spiral were strolling around Edinburgh Zoo. He was not impressed.

"There were a lot more animals when I came here last," he grumped. "Looks like they moved a bunch out to make way for play areas, cafés and gift shops."

"Is this your way of saying you want to go on safari?"

"God, no." he pressed his face against the glass of the ape enclosure. "All these countries have left is mosquitos and monkeys that give you Ebola."

"Only if you shag them."

"Well… we might fall out." He raised an eyebrow. "Hey. What about Australia?"

"Yeah. No."

"Shame. I always wanted to drive the Great Ocean Road and see those big rock formations. I've got a postcard with their picture."

"You mean the Twelve Apostles near Port Campbell?" Dark looked smug. "I took a helicopter flight over that."

"You did?" Spiral was impressed.

"They warned me not to fiddle with the door, which had honestly never occurred to me."

"Why not? Was it held on with Scotch tape?"

"Exactly. It kind of spoiled my enjoyment of the trip, especially when the helicopter flew sideways to let me see straight down. I wondered if having my face squashed against the glass by centrifugal forces counted as fiddling with the door."

Dark gave a wry grin.

"The pilot told me there were only ever nine formations, and one of *them* fell down. Probably because he flew into it. At one point, he was holding the joystick with his teeth while he searched his bag for a sandwich. He also said they used to be called the Sow and Piglets."

"Why change the name to the Twelve Apostles?"

"Because tourists wouldn't pay money to see an attraction called the Sow and Piglets."

"That's Australia out, then. Any suggestions?"

"I'd *really* like to go to America," Dark replied with bated breath. "After Scotland, it was next on my bucket list."

"You have a bucket list?" Spiral screwed up his face.

"I started making it when I was in that damned helicopter."

"OK, then." He took her hand. "Why don't we rent a car and drive from one side of the USA to the other? We got the money and the time. Now we're officially unemployed, that is."

"For real?"

"Totally." Spiral nudged her. "Unless you wanna get a static caravan in Skegness. I hear it's got a great fish and chip shop."

Dark launched herself into his arms.

"Spiral Wood?" she squealed. "I fucking love you."

Callan Loch 2024

Dark and Lachlan

A horn honked outside. Dark dropped Spiral's book on the bed and looked out of the window. It was Lachlan.

She closed her eyes for a second, trying to banish the thought of Spiral from her mind. Then she ran outside and got into his car.

"Where are we going?"

"Tae sit on top of Ben Afton and have a wee picnic."

"I hope he's a friend of yours or that'll get awkward pretty quick."

"Very witty."

"Is it high up?"

"Yes. It's a mountain."

"Wait here."

Dark ran back inside and came back with a large duffle bag, which she threw into the boot.

"What's that?"

"You'll see." Dark tapped a finger to her nose.

"Woman of mystery. You certainly fit in well here." Lachlan put the car in gear and drove away.

After 20 minutes, a huge purple peak rose in front of them.

"Are we going to be trudging up some cliff face, surrounded by swarms of biting insects?" Dark inquired hesitantly. "I'm a bit out of shape."

"Nice try, but I've seen you naked." Lachlan glanced at her as if he was reaffirming the statement. "Dinnae worry. There's a car park a couple of thousand feet up. I'm not lugging a picnic basket over this hill, nae matter how shapely you are.".

"Oh." Dark fell silent as the car began to chug up a steep incline.

"Great view, eh?" Lachlan glanced at her again. "Why have you got your eyes closed?"

"I have a thing about cars and steep hills," she replied nervously. "Are we there yet?"

"That's the best thing about road trips," he laughed. "You find out all sorts of interesting stuff aboot your passenger."

"No talking. Concentrate on the road."

"Seriously. Are you all right?"

"Fine." Dark kept her head down. "Just making a new bucket list."

Dark and Lachlan sat on a stone outcrop, the nearby wicker basket holding down a Mexican blanket. Lachlan had set out sandwiches, chicken legs, grapes, cheese, crackers and pear juice.

Below them, a gorse and heather scree plunged to a green valley with a small loch at the bottom, sparkling in the sunlight. On the other side, an array of golden peaks stretched into the distance.

"This was worth getting scared shitless for." Dark bit into a chicken leg. "It's a sensational place to live."

"It is indeed." Lachlan was staring intently at her.

"What? Do I have grease on my chin?"

"I said I dinnae want to know aboot your ex but I have tae admit, I'm intrigued by why he might have chosen to end up in a place like this. As I said, I dinnae even ken his name but..."

"Neither did I," Dark replied instinctively, then mentally kicked herself. Lachlan looked suitably confused.

The cat was out of the bag now. She fell back into the old tactic of vagueness.

"He called himself various things," she half explained. "Was into some dodgy stuff, you see."

"I dinnae think I like this guy," Lachlan grunted. "But he obviously weighs heavily on your mind."

Dark was going to change the subject. Yet, if she couldn't open up to Lachlan, who could she bare her soul to?

"He wasn't a villain or anything," she insisted. "He was actually an incredible person. Let's just say he had a wonky moral compass and often operated on the wrong side of the law."

She knew how that sounded and expected a sarcastic comment but Lachlan merely indicated for her to go on.

"I don't know what else to tell you."

"Sum him up in one sentence." Lachlan folded his arms. "You're good at that."

What could she tell him? That Spiral was a man of massive contradictions? A serial complainer who couched every grievance as a witticism? A deeply dissatisfied and serious man who acted as if life was a joke? A sad and empty person who covered up a well of loneliness by being entertaining?

Dark had tried never to think of Spiral in any of those terms before. Yet, in hindsight, they seemed so obvious, especially when compared to Lachlan.

Tears sprang, unbidden, to her eyes.

"He was a notorious liar," she said eventually. "A guy you experienced rather than understood."

"That's two sentences. You must hae really loved him."

"I did." She wiped wet cheeks. "Until he fucked off without telling me why."

"Hell, Dark." Lachlan was shocked. "You dinnae actually know that he left you. If he was intae dodgy stuff, maybe he was kidnapped or something."

It seemed an odd thing to assume but she let it go.

"No, he always landed on his feet. We fought and he left to pull off some stupid last job. If he had really loved me, he would have come back. I'm still processing that."

"I didnae mean tae upset you." Lachlan reached out and took her hand. "I apologise. Besides, I've done a few dubious things in my life, so I cannae criticise."

"Have you ever been in love?" It was time to change the subject, Dark thought. She'd already said too much.

"I loved a girl once," Lachlan replied. "Ewa Jakubowicz. I never could pronounce the name properly, so she called herself Eva Stone. She used to clean for me, Big Don and a couple of other big properties around Aftonhouse."

"I think Elspeth Cameron mentioned someone like that. No specifics, though."

"Ewa was a very private person. Didnae even want people tae know we were together."

"A couple of enigmatic hermits, eh? Sounds like a good match."

"We both had our reasons for being reclusive," Lachlan said softly. "It's in the past now."

"What happened to her? Elspeth said she left around the same time as Billy."

"Aye, she did. And I don't know where she is either." He tightened his grip on Dark's hand. "Listen. Talking about the past seems difficult for both of us, so it's my turn to change the subject."

"All right."

"Ehmmmm… Tell me a film you've cried at."

"That's nicely random." Dark thought for a moment. "I cried at *Robin of Sherwood*."

"Why did you cry at that?" Lachlan looked puzzled. "Was it the terrible theme song?"

"It was the bit where the woman was having a baby and Kevin Costner came along and pulled it out of her stomach."

"And it made you cry? I dinnae even remember that part."

"Yup. I was in a bar and I sobbed for two hours."

"That's a lot of sobbing."

"I got really, really drunk and cried and cried and cried… I don't… I think I was crying about something else… I don't know why I was crying. People eventually came up and bought me drinks and asked me what the matter was."

"OK. Tell me a film that you cried at because of the film."

"It *was* because of the film."

"But the movie wasn't real."

"Then you… suspend your disbelief to become part of the fantasy." She picked at a grass frond. "And sometimes you just need to cry."

"I understand that."

"My turn." Dark brightened. "You say you travel a lot. Where have you never visited that you'd love to go."

"The USA." His reply was instant. "Been dying to see it ever since I was a kid but never managed to crack the market. Have you been there?"

"Yes." Her reply was so curt, Lachlan was wise enough not to press it.

"What about you?" He put his arm round her. "Scotland's about as far from Australia as you can get. Why come here of all places?"

Dark recalled Spiral asking her the same question on their first night together. This time, she decided to tell the truth.

"My dad was Scottish. He moved to Australia to become a failed writer and succeeded splendidly at it. I seem to have inherited his talent."

"You two are close?"

"He walked out on mum and me when I was a teenager. I rarely spoke to him after that. Don't much like to talk about him."

"I wasnae intending tae pry."

Dark looked at Lachlan evenly.

"He's the reason I came here," she said, finally. "I guess I'm more like dad than I realised."

Australia 2022

Dark and Her Father

Dark sat in a rented car and stared at her father's house. It was an old wooden Queenslander perched on the edge of a cliff, with extensions added to make it look more modern. Suited him more than he probably realised. Or maybe he did. Paul Arrowsmith was a perceptive sort when it suited him.

She got out and rang the doorbell.

"I'm roond the back," an Aberdonian voice shouted. Despite years in Australia, her father had never lost his original accent.

He was standing on the patio, leaning casually against a pillar. Despite the heat, he had on a shirt, tie, chinos and boots. His grey hair was neatly combed, though it was much thinner than the last time she had seen him. Mind you, that had been five years ago when he had paid her an impromptu visit. The reception had been a frosty one and he quickly left again.

"This is a pleasant surprise." He made to hug Dark, but her look put him off. He indicated a pitcher on a Venetian-style tiled table instead. "Hae a drink."

"Dark poured herself a tumbler.

"If you dinnae mind…" he slowly lowered himself onto a rattan chair. "Got a few back problems."

Dark sat as well, taking a sip. She detected a hint of rum in whatever the concoction was.

"I've got to say, I was pretty shocked when you emailed to tell me you were coming." He bit his lip. "Is everything all right?"

"I was going to ask you the same question."

"Why wouldn't I be?"

"Because you transferred $80,000 into my bank account a few days ago."

She studied her dad's face. There were deep lines on his forehead and bags under his eyes, yet he was still a good looking man.

"I'm fine," he said. "It's a tax dodge."

"Hmmm."

"I presume you didnae fly up here to thank me."

"It was my fiancé's idea. He thinks you and I should try to patch things up."

"Congratulations. I didnae ken you were tae be wed."

"But you knew my bank details?"

"Got them from your Auntie May," he winked. "I would have asked her to pass the money on to you personally but I dinnae trust that scunner with so much cash. Getting hitched, eh?"

"Arthur thinks you should be at the wedding. He's an old-fashioned sort. Values family."

"*Arthur?*"

"Don't even start."

"Sorry." Paul held up his hands. "Your mum winnae want me there."

"Too right. Not sure I do either."

"Well, this visit is going swimmingly."

They silently concentrated on their drinks for a few moments.

"I dinnae ken what I'm supposed to say." Paul's eyes darted around as if he were afraid to look at his daughter.

"If you're going to go, I'll have to plead your case to mum. As far as she's concerned, you dumped us for a young blonde and that's that."

"You think there's mair tae it?"

"I've never asked for your side of the story."

"Nothing I say will work with your mother," he grunted. "Just tell her I fucked up, as always, and I'm sorry."

"Then I apologise for wasting your time." Dark made to rise.

"Unless, of course, it's actually *you* who wants to know," Paul said quickly.

"Give it your best shot. Just don't expect my forgiveness."

"I'm no looking for forgiveness. I dinnae even expect you to understand."

"Try me."

"All right." He fumbled in his pocket and took out a cigarette packet. "What dae you think of your mum?"

"She's the kindest and most loving person I've ever met. The sort that genuinely wants to make the world a better place."

"Yeah," Paul grunted. "Unfortunately, she decided tae practise on me."

"Not helping your case, father."

"I hae plenty of shortcomings, aye. I'm prickly and never sure of myself, so I cover it up with fake arrogance. But I assumed your mum thought my good points outweighed the bad ones. At one time, we were both pretty wild, you know."

"Mum?" Dark laughed. "Wild? You're kidding."

"Oh, aye. I used to remind her of all the crazy times we had. Her answer always horrified me."

"I'll bite. What did she say?"

"She said I was looking at the past through rose-tinted glasses. That the bad times always outweighed the good ones." He fished a lighter from his pocket and lit his cigarette. "I felt she was rewriting our history with me as the villain."

"You didn't agree?"

"I'd tried my best tae change and be the good guy but I soon discovered what happens to them." He took a long drag on his cigarette. "They get walked over."

"I'm sure it's a bit more complicated than that."

"Must hae been, cause *I* couldnae understand." He took another sip of his drink and coughed. "Other people thought I was funny and smart and good-natured but she said it was because they hadnae spent enough time with me. I presumed she included you in that explanation, which frightened the hell oot of me."

He gave a lopsided grin.

"I decided to gie her theory a go and moved out."

"Bollocks." Dark gave a bark of laughter. "You abandoned mum for some young blonde."

"You cannae abandon someone who doesn't need you, Dorothy," Paul chuckled. "Julie lasted about ten minutes. The grass may be greener on the other side of the hill but, at my age, I was finding it difficult to even get over the hill."

He fumbled for another cigarette and lit it.

"But I made friends here and they *didnae* get tired of me. They accept who I am. We see bands, go to the theatre, read books, travel and visit bars. We hae conversations aboot art, politics and music, not schools, lawns and zoning permits."

"Or your child, apparently." Tears stung her eyes. "*I* needed you, dad."

"I reached out many times, Dorothy. You didnae want tae know."

"I was hurt!"

"And I was everything your mother claimed. Too selfish and paranoid to handle rejection." He exhaled a bitter worm of smoke. So, aye. The money is an apology. I figured you could see a wee bit of the world before you got too old or tied down. You've never been anywhere."

"I went to Bundaberg once. It was shut."

"Scotland would be the perfect place to start." Her father ignored the sarcasm. "I miss it, you know. But I never kept in touch with anyone there, so it's too late now. Better I gie *you* that opportunity."

"I'm engaged to be married, remember?"

"Bring him with you. I sent enough."

"He'd never do something like that," Dark laughed. "He's got a job and we've planned the ceremony."

"Tell him to take vacation time and put off the nuptials until you get back."

"He's… he… He loves me but he'd never allow it."

Paul stared at her.

"No," Dark snapped. "You do *not* get to do this."

"Sorry. It's your life. Buy a Kia or something. Get new decking and a shade sail for the hoose."

"You're impossible."

"And you turned out as smart and wonderful as I could hae wished," Paul grinned. "I must have done something right."

"Leaving wasn't it, if you're trying to validate your actions."

"Well beyond that, baby. But I may have to gie the wedding a pass. You dinnae need your mum and I slugging it oot in the reception area."

He stubbed out his second cigarette.

"So, tomorrow? You want tae do lunch?" He gave a shy smile. "You could stay here tonight, you ken. Instead of some hotel. Talk aboot things that dinnae make us feel shit."

"I'm flying out tonight, dad. I just thought I should say thank you for the money in person."

"Oh." Her father blinked. "OK. I didnae realise."

He loosened his tie.

"Look. I'll go if it's something you really want. I mean, I would love to. I just didn't think you'd appreciate it. That you felt… y'know… obligated. Not that you should."

For the first time, Dark got a sense of how truly alone he was.

"We've got a few months," she relented. "How about I come back on my next vacation time and stay longer? I'll work on mum and we can talk about it then."

"Aye. Aye, that would be awesome."

He leaned forwards and took her hand. His sleeves slid up, revealing liver spots.

"Dorothy. Words cannae describe what this means to me. Or how sorry I am."

"I suppose I'm glad I came, then." Dark stood up. "Maybe this is the beginning of a beginning, eh?"

"Absolutely. I'll see you to the car." Paul tried to rise, then sank again, wincing. "Sorry. Like I said. Got a bit of a hip problem these days."

"I thought it was your back?"

"Both," he laughed. "Price of living it large, toots,"

"You rest, then. Gotta keep your strength up if we're going to be going to bars and theatres and having conversations about art and philosophy."

"Can I give you one piece of philosophical advice?"

"I suppose."

"Everything is complicated and an intelligent person recognises and accepts that. Yet, sometimes it does a body good tae just sum things up in one sentence."

"And what's your sentence."

"Life is too short tae waste a second, so cram as much in as you can." He was wracked by a fit of coughing. "Dorothy?"

"Yes?"

"I do love you. Please believe that."

She hesitated.

"I love you too, dad."

Paul Arrowsmith died of cancer three weeks later.

Callan Loch 2024

Dark and Lachlan

"Oh, Christ," Lachlan paled. "I'm so sorry."

"Turns out his body was riddled with tumours," Dark said. "He knew, of course. I guess he didn't want me to mistake pity for love."

"And the fiancée?"

"Dumped him for being too dull and controlling. I am my father's daughter, after all."

"At least you two were close at the end."

"Closer than you think. I brought his ashes with me."

"You took him home. Well done." Lachlan nodded approvingly. "Where dae you intend to scatter them?"

"I was going to pick the place where he grew up in Aberdeen but, apparently, it's a car park." She looked around. "This might be as good a place as any. It's beautiful enough."

"That would be beyond ironic," Lachlan said apprehensively. "Don't take this the wrong way but I brought you to Callan Loch for a reason. Not just a picnic."

"Want to elaborate?"

"Tae introduce you to my mum, in a weird way."

"I don't understand. We're in the middle of nowhere."

"My mum and brother died in this glen. Trapped in a snowstorm."

"Fuck, Lachlan." Dark squeezed his hand. "I don't know what to say."

"Like your dad, it's not something I'm comfortable talking aboot. At least, not yet. But I come here a lot."

"Thank you for bringing me."

"Well, this conversation has certainly taken a turn for the maudlin." Lachlan rested his chin on the crook of one knee. "Cheer me up, Dark. Say something irreverent. I don't care what. Break the spell."

"All right." She leaned across and kissed him. "What football team do you support? Ever had a deep-fried Mars Bar? Favourite subject at school?"

She nudged him.

"Do you like to be on top or below? Ever made a booty call?"

"No tae the last one." He winked at her. "But I'm definitely considering it."

"Then wait a couple of nights," Dark smiled. "I've got to get some work done on this stupid magazine article. Then I'm all yours."

"Deal. Shall we go?"

"Yeah."

Dark helped him load the picnic remains back into the car. Then she pulled out the duffle bag.

"Drive down the mountain for a mile or two," she said. "I'll be along shortly."

"Are your father's ashes in there?" Lachlan looked perturbed.

"No. They're at home."

"You can't walk down. It'll take forever."

"Not walking. Trust me. Yeah?"

"Ehhhh... All right." He got into the car, shot her a puzzled look and drove off.

After a few minutes, Lachlan parked on the grass verge and got out of the vehicle. After a few minutes, he heard a yell and looked up.

In the distance, Dark was hurtling down the winding road on a skateboard, hair flying behind her and skirt flapping.

"Holy Mother of Christ." Lachlan opened the glove compartment, pulled out a pair of binoculars and trained them on the woman. "You're going tae kill yourself."

Dark executed a perfect turn on a hairpin bend and continued downhill. Her mouth was open in a silent scream, face betraying both elation and terror. All at once, she seemed to be a child testing her limits and an adult trying to break free of some earthly bond.

"What a fucking woman," Lachlan breathed.

As Dark approached at breakneck speed, he tossed the binoculars back into his car and stood in the middle of the road, ready to catch her.

She tipped up the front of the skateboard, ground to a halt and skipped into his arms.

"Ta-dah!"

"You are properly mental." Lachlan held her tight. "How do you know how to do that?"

"Heaven on a half-pipe, I was." She kissed his lips. "Some things you never forget."

"I dinnae ken about that. Last few moments there, I forgot how tae breathe."

"That's another one on my bucket list ticked off," she beamed. "Skateboard down a mountain."

"I thought you were terrified of hills."

"I am. That's the whole point."

"Shit." Lachlan buried his head in her shoulder and closed his eyes. "I'm scared of them as well, now."

He dropped Dark off and kissed her passionately before he left.

"So you dinnae forget," he grinned.

"That's not likely." She made her way into the cottage, her knees weak. Damn, but he was sexy.

"Took me to meet your dead mum," she muttered to herself. "That's both genuinely touching and truly disturbing."

USA 2024

Dark and Spiral

Dark made herself a sandwich and watched TV until bedtime. The jotter was still lying on the covers.

Spiral's Notebook. Get it?

He had presented his journal to her when they got back from their American holiday and she had read it many times.

Lying on the bed, she opened the book once more.

USA Trip

I've decided to keep a diary of our drive across America. I write a lot. Shopping lists. Christmas cards. I write to wicked uncles. When I was little, I lost my dog and designed **Have u Seen Sparky?** *posters, with an eloquent piece underneath about how much I missed him. I didn't have a photo, so I pasted on a picture from some glossy magazine and got a better-looking pet back. That's how I first learned the power of advertising. And how to con.*

It all comes from my Granddad. His efforts to be a famous screenwriter may have been hampered by living in the silent era, but he was a pioneer of subliminal adverts.

Help! I'm tied to the railroad tracks
(buy a hot dog)

Subdue phobia about flying long enough to board a plane with Dark for New York. Manage to keep the aircraft airborne the whole way by sheer force of will and pulling up on the seat arms - forcing me to stay awake through two showings of Love Actually.

Repeat over and over the statistically dubious fact that I'm more likely to be kicked to death by a donkey than killed in an air crash. Trouble is, I'm actually on a plane and I've never been within ten feet of a donkey. Dark reminds me of my promise to ride one down the Grand Canyon.

Now I have two things to be petrified about.

Lunch in Times Square. Tell the waiter of our intended adventure to fly to San Francisco and drive back.

"We're going through Death Valley." Dark gives him a manic grin.

"In this heat?" He puts down a plate of fries that looks like it might take two days to cross. "Your tyres will melt and you'll die."

Dark argues we should take the long way around, while I am more desperate than ever to go through it.

She wins.

Visit St Patrick's Cathedral in Manhattan. It has a giant video screen that plays The Exorcist. *All right, that's not true, but I did put it in the suggestion box. What it does have is a bunch of choirboys singing right in the middle, surrounded by shafts of light - enough to make me come over all knish and religious. There are also priests everywhere.*

I think shafting is a definite theme in that place.

Fly to San Francisco next morning and take a cable car to Pacific Heights. Discover Dark is afraid of being in vehicles on inclines. As well as being genuinely bizarre, this does not bode well for crossing the Rockies.

Rent bright red Mustang Convertible. It's the kind of car owned by middle-aged women who have just gone through their fourth divorce. Ask where we can drop it in New York.

"Nobody's ever rented a car to drive that far." The woman behind the desk looks at her computer. "Apparently, we have an office someplace called... eh... Green Witch Village. But you'll probably want to go the whole way into the city."

She gives us a fold-out brochure.

"Have a nice day."

"This is a map of Arlington Cemetery."

"That's all I got."

Leave California, drive through Yosemite Park, then Mohave Desert (avoiding Death Valley). As compensation, I put the top down and manage to get the Mustang up to 160 miles an hour, until Dark tries to throttle me - which takes all her strength as she is pinned to the seat by G-forces. As we approach Las Vegas, her excitement level goes off the scale and I begin to believe Elvis might really be alive.

THERE ARE REAL LIONS IN THE CASINO!!!!
I tell the keeper, "Hey, you can't just leave that lion there." He doesn't laugh. Maybe he heard it before.

Stay at the Luxor Hotel. Dark leans over the balcony in her bathrobe and waves to people while I take her from behind. They must think she's truly pleased to see them.

This is a great holiday and I am totally in love with her.

All day drive across Arizona. Abandon the Interstate and take Route 66. Route 66!!!! Unfortunately, it's now pitch black, and I'm exhausted because we stayed up all night in Las Vegas. I get my kicks by trying to stay on Route 66 and not end up embedding the car in a giant cactus.

Grand Canyon is the greatest thing I have ever seen! But there is no fence and Dark keeps wandering onto ledges, hundreds of feet up, while looking through her camera viewfinder. Spend the day with my eyes shut and miss most of the scenery.

Across Utah to reach Monument Valley at sunset. Everything is red and gold and awe-inspiring. Feel like John Wayne, only several inches shorter. Sensation fades as we run out of gas in the tiny town of Mexican Hat and check into a seedy motel populated by beefy bikers with large white moustaches. Wonder why they don't just call the place Sombrero but too afraid to ask.

Through Colorado on the interstate to Denver. Download all the Grand Canyon pictures onto my laptop, then overwrite them by mistake.
First fight of the holiday.

Drive towards the Rockies. Dark is so distracted by my pointing and yelling at the mountains she gets pulled over for speeding. Never seen her so quiet. Perhaps it's the fact that the policeman won't take his hand off his gun. He asks her if she's ever seen The Golden Girls.
"Yes. No. I don't know. Do you want me to?"
"There was a Dorothy in that."
"Oh. Hahahahahaha."
Not wanting to deal with someone who is obviously insane, he lets us go.
"Thank God I wasn't driving," I say.
"Why not?"
"I don't have a licence."
Dark is so annoyed, she drives up 12,000 feet and over the Rocky Mountain National Park before remembering she is scared of hills.

Wake up in Cheyenne, Wyoming. How the hell did we end up in Cheyenne? Dark takes 40 pictures of the Kum and Go gas station because she thinks it's funny. Discover you can't buy wine anywhere in the American interior. Except for something called Arbour Mist, which isn't really wine and tastes like sick.

Across Nebraska on Interstate 80. Breakfast at a giant truck stop where the non-smoking section is one table next to the toilet. Have discovered I need to use a toned-down version of my accent so the locals understand me. In Iowa, a motel clerk compliments me on my grasp of English.

Across Indiana on Interstate 80. Car radio will only play soft rock, country and western, God channels and rants about the Democrats. For light relief, we detour into Amish country and are warned not to take photographs. If they don't want their pictures taken, why the hell are they so damned stylish in their muted greys and hipster beards? See one using an electric lawnmower and give her the evil eye.

Stop in Omaha on Interstate 80. Now I know why they named a beach covered in dead Americans after it. Still, we manage to find an Afghani restaurant that has authentic belly dancers. Halfway through dessert, we're invaded by the Russian restaurant next door.

Stop at Inner Space Caverns. Fantastic place. They have a little stream outside and will sell you a bag of dirt for $5.00 - so you can pan for jewels like the old-time diggers - the ones who starved to death in their thousands. The caverns themselves are exceptional. Did you know it takes a stalactite over 100 years to grow an inch? I sympathize.

The cavern tour, however, is amazingly bad. At one point, we have a light show, which consists of switching off the lights and then switching them back on. Meanwhile, a loudspeaker tells us how great God was for creating the caverns. Dark is tickled pink and I'm sure

God is too. It's undeniably easier than bothering to figure out how the various rock formations were actually formed.

Best part of the tour is a kid called Curtis. Every time the guide (who has a speech impediment) invites questions, Curtis asks, "What's that?" and points at a large rock. This invites the inevitable reply. "Ith a large rock."

TOUR GUIDE
The cave paintingth represent the kind of animalth whose fothilized remaineth were found in the cave over the yearth.

GERMAN TOURIST
Zey are superb, zo not as good as ze ones ve have at ze Buttfelchin caves in my homeland. It is remarkable how new and shiny zey are.

TOUR GUIDE
They were redone with gloth paint a couple of yearth ago. Thith ith a camel. Ath you can thee, it only hath one hump, unlike the camelth today.

CURTIS
That camel's got two humps.

TOUR GUIDE
It wathn't very well retouched

CURTIS
Dromedaries have just one hump. They're camels today.

TOUR GUIDE
And thith is a big rock. Any more questionth?

CURTIS

Where'th the rethtroomth?

Stay in Red Roof Motel, Ohio. Larry, the motel clerk, asks if I have definitive proof that the Loch Ness Monster exists. Well… not on me. I suspect he has a picture of Norman Bates in his office. We are then kept awake all night by what sounds like the Loch Ness Monster. In the morning, we find it was a bullfrog the size of a grape.

Through Ohio on Interstate 80. Through Pennsylvania on Interstate 80. Begin to hate Interstate 80. Take photograph of dead deer.

Reach Chicago and end up in a piano bar at two in the morning with a guy in a tux asking for requests. Dark, being Australian, requests Land Down Under. *The guy plays it. For a laugh, I request* Now I Wanna Sniff Some Glue *by the Ramones. He plays it.*

Next night we go to a Beat Poetry open mike night at the Lizard Lounge and discover they really do wear black polo necks. Any shred of importance I ever attached to the Beat Generation is now gone. There are types of people who should never take themselves seriously but always do… Members of Oasis. Women in dungarees. Anyone from France. Beat poets.

Detour to Philadelphia and have dinner at a fancy gay Cuban restaurant before visiting the ballet. Have raw sea bass for the first time. Delicious. Just think how good it would have tasted if someone had cooked it. Cuba and gayness go well together - all those leather, tight trousers and moustaches. They just don't go well together in Cuba.

At the ballet, they play a Philip Glass number, which I think is great cause the piano player gives me something to watch. Perhaps we shouldn't have sat at the front, where the thump, thump of large dancers landing detracts from the magic a little. All the same, they take fifteen encores.

I think anyone who works hard should join hands and take a bow when they're done. Would look great on building sites.

Reach New York in one piece. To celebrate, we go to see American Idiot: The Musical - *where nicely dressed white families enjoy a Broadway musical written by a punk rock band about the dark side of the American dream. This country doesn't do irony but I love it. Except for Interstate 80.*

Go to Coney Island. It's raining, everything is closed and the 8th Street boardwalk is almost deserted. I sing a few verses of On the Boardwalk *and Dark dances. Then it's completely deserted.*

Finally, we get a cab to JFK. When the Pakistani driver finally understands my directions, he compliments me on my grasp of English.

Thank you for a wonderful time, Dark. I want to go all sorts of places with you. Europe. Asia. Even Australia, someday. So many possibilities.

Last night I couldn't sleep for dreaming.
XXXX

Dark closed the journal and lay back. That was Spiral all over. Always plotting the next move. Rushing across America in search of a new destination rather than savouring the moment. Seeing incredible things, yet driven to make them even more fantastical. Once, she had thought his embellishments of what really happened were whimsical and fun.

Now she realised nothing was quite enough for Spiral Wood. Truth was never as good as fantasy and so he tried to morph what was real into what he imagined it could be.

She suspected now that this included her.

Perhaps it was Lachlan's fault. Perhaps not. Yet, slowly but surely, Dark was beginning to see Spiral Wood in a different light.

-Part IV-

Someone I loved once gave me
a box full of darkness.
It took me years to understand
that this, too, was a gift.
Mary Oliver. *The Uses of Sorrow*

Merchiston Point 2023

Lachlan and Billy

Lachlan and Billy pulled the big white truck onto a rutted track winding between rocky outcrops. A short way from Merchiston Point, the track veered steeply left and downhill.

"Let me off," Lachlan said. "There's a fine view fae here and plenty places tae hide."

He got out and Billy carried on, finally stopping the van next to a small cove with a rocky beach. A motor yacht was moored one hundred yards offshore and a dingy with an outboard motor soon left it and chugged towards land. Two men jumped out, ignoring the icy water, and pulled the craft to shore. Then they strode towards Billy.

Both were brawny, with thick necks and shaved heads. One had a scar running from forehead to chin, and the other carried a plastic case. There was no greeting or shaking of hands.

"Take a walk and do not look back." The leading man jerked his thumb up the track.

"You will not return until our boat is gone," the other added curtly.

Both had thick Eastern European accents and their aggressive stance indicated they would brook no argument.

"Here is your money." The leader unfastened his bag and showed Billy. It was stuffed with cash. He opened the truck's driver door and threw it inside.

"There. Now, move to the top of the hill and wait until you hear the engine of our boat fade away. If we see you again before we leave, we will kill you."

"Keep your hair on," Billy replied belligerently. "I'm going."

He trudged back to the rocky outcrop. Once he had rounded it, he ducked out of sight. Lachlan was above him, wedged between two boulders.

"That pair aren't any of our usual contacts," Billy whispered. "Don't recognise the boat either."

"This gets better and better."

"It must be freezing on the water, but they're wearing short puffer jackets and no gloves."

"So what?" Lachlan glanced down at him. "They look hard enough tae headbutt a whale."

"It means they have guns tucked into the waistbands of their jeans. Easier to reach, that way."

"I'm scared tae ask how you even ken that."

"Keep well hidden. Let's not do anything to antagonise them."

"They looked pretty annoyed by the fact that you even exist."

"Pity you didn't bring more lunch. I could murder a Mars Bar right now." Billy lay back. "What are they up to?"

"They've opened the back door of the truck and one is climbing inside." Lachlan peered down the sight of his rifle. Then his head shot up.

"Billy?"

"What?"

"There's someone inside. It looks like they're bound and gagged." Lachlan gritted his teeth. "Have we been fucking people trafficking, Bill? Is that what Big Don has gotten us mixed up in?"

"Even my father wouldn't stoop that low. And you don't traffic just one person."

"Then it's a kidnapping. I'm going to try and get closer to…"

"Fuck, no." Billy jumped up. "I'm not going to be party to something like this. You stay here."

Before Lachlan could object, he marched down towards the vehicle.

Cameron's Store 2024

Dark, Elspeth and Frankie

"**T**he article is written."

Dark was in Frankie and Elspeth Cameron's flat. She had invited herself and the women seemed pleased by that. They really must be starved of company. Just in case, she had brought four bottles of wine and a bag of Quality Street chocolates.

"Oooh. Let's see it, then." Elspeth poured them all glasses.

Dark handed over her laptop. She had spent most of the last two days writing her piece, using large dollops of Wikipedia and a second-hand book on the area she had cribbed. She was slightly apprehensive but, then again, who looked up the place they lived? Besides, she had actually made a serious effort to make it entertaining.

Frankie and Dark finished reading and nodded approvingly.

"This is very good. And the store got a namecheck."

"Of course." Dark felt remorseful about that. After all, the thing was never actually going to be published.

"We sorely need this," Frankie said gratefully. "If we don't get more foot traffic, we're going to have to close down."

"The hotel and restaurant are in dire straits too," Elspeth added. "Aftonhouse is dying on its feet."

Now Dark felt a lot worse.

"I take it you'll be heading back to Edinburgh soon." Elspeth looked a little crestfallen.

"I'm not sure," Dark said. "I can email the article, so it's not like I have to rush. I…eh…"

"You've fallen in love with the place and don't want to leave?"

"I've been spending quite a bit of time with Lachlan Robertson. Might stick around for a few days. My landlady doesn't have any other bookings."

Elspeth and Frankie glanced at each other.

"You mean you're sleeping with him." Frankie waggled grey eyebrows.

"Mother!"

"We didn't do much sleeping," Dark grinned.

"You pair are as bad as each other." Elspeth helped herself to a chocolate. "But I'm glad for you,"

"He's a complex man with a tragic past," Frankie agreed. "Deserves some happiness."

"Are you talking about his mum and brother?" Dark asked. "He said they died in a snowstorm but didn't elaborate."

"If Lachlan hasn't told her, then it's honestly not our place…" Elspeth began.

"It's not something he talks about. But he should." Frankie cut her off. "I saw the effect it had on him."

"Can you enlighten me in any way?" Dark pleaded. "What exactly happened?"

"When Lachie was seventeen, the Robertson farm was much bigger than it is now. It was a pretty harsh winter, so when there was a break in the weather, his mum took Lachie and his little brother in a land buggy to check on the sheep."

"They got caught in a sudden snowstorm, miles from anywhere." Elspeth could see there was no deterring her mother. "Lachie's mum skidded onto a small frozen loch and the buggy went through the ice. They got out alive but they were soaked and it was below freezing."

"Lachlan ran seven miles through the blizzard until he got to Gordon Crabbe's house," Frankie continued. "He called Highland Rescue but drifts had already covered Lachie's mum and brother. By the time the helicopter finally found them, it was too late."

Dark put a hand to her mouth.

"Lachie and his father always had a strained relationship and that was the last straw," Elspeth sighed. "Lachlan moved in with mum but he'd turned wild, working with Billy Milne for Big Don and getting into all sorts of trouble. Meanwhile, his dad sold everything but the farmhouse and began drinking and taking drugs. Died of an overdose not long after."

"His father blamed Lachie for their deaths, you see," Frankie continued. "It wasn't until he was gone that Lachlan calmed down. Moved into the property and became pretty much a recluse."

She poured herself another glass.

"Billy took that pretty hard. He depended on Lachie to stand up to..."

"No, mum." Elspeth put a hand on her arm. "That's enough."

"She's not a reporter now, dear. She's our friend."

Dark nodded assent.

"I said no." A steely tone crept into Elspeth's voice. "That's Lachlan's story to tell, should he wish to."

"But he can't, can he?" the older woman objected. "He's not..."

"Enough!" her daughter barked.

"Sorry. I've got a big mouth." Frankie looked abashed. "Add a couple of glasses of wine and I'm anybody's."

"You are something else, Frankie!" Dark burst out laughing. "I knew I'd like you."

"Good. In that case, I have a couple of favours to ask."

"Name them."

"I was wondering if you might put my daughter up in Edinburgh for a few days, once you do go back. She could do with seeing a bit more of life."

"Mother!" Elspeth went red.

Dark was about to make an excuse. Yet, she felt sorry for the girl, and after all, they got on well.

"I don't mind," she said. "But I'll tell you something. I've had a few crazy adventures before I got here. Done some pretty wild things, which I won't elaborate on."

She picked her way carefully.

"It was great. I don't deny it. But so is this place. There's a part of me that wants to slow down and enjoy peace and stability."

Spiral and Lachlan sprang into her mind.

"Being on the roller coaster is a rush. Lights flash. Your heart pounds. Your senses are in a whirl. But everything is a blur and you don't properly take it in."

She took a deep breath.

"So, part of you is *really* glad when it's over."

"I bet you've given that little speech to yourself a dozen times." Frankie mused. "This might be the first time you've genuinely believed it."

"*Mum*!"

"No." Dark nodded. "She's absolutely right. And the second favour?"

"And I'd like you to come pick me up tomorrow morning," Frankie said. "I have something to show you."

"I've already had a look around."

"This one's off the beaten track. With an interesting story attached."

"Fair enough."

It was after midnight when Dark got her usual taxi home. Usually, she sat in silence at the back. This time, she got into the passenger side.

"What's your name?" she asked the driver.

"George Manning." He sounded surprised and pleased at being asked.

"You have an English accent. What are you doing up here?"

"I'm from Leeds originally," he said. "Came up on holiday twenty years ago and took to the place. So, me and Dianne took a chance and moved here."

"Dianne is your wife?"

"Married for nearly half a century now. Epic woman. We've got two kids, Jacob and Noah."

"Tell me about them."

And they gossiped all the way home.

Milne Mansion 2024

Dark and Frankie

The next morning, Dark picked Frankie up and drove west out of Aftonhouse.

"Take this turning," she pointed after a few minutes. Dark followed the road until it came to a massive house on a hill. In the distance, she could see Spiral Wood, a cornucopia of leaves glistening in the morning dew.

Despite the grandeur, the building was obviously abandoned. Grass grew high on the lawns and the windows were boarded up. Frankie stared at it for a while.

"You remind me of myself when I was younger, kid," she said finally. "I don't know if it's a good thing."

Dark was smart enough not to comment on that observation.

"So, did some historic event take place in this mansion?"

"It belonged to Big Don Milne." Frankie continued. "Elspeth told me you talked about him and Billy."

"It wasn't for my story. We were just shooting the breeze."

"Writing articles is a good job, I imagine." Frankie turned to face her. "But don't you ever want to tell a proper tale? A novel, perhaps?"

"It's crossed my mind. You giving me a pep talk?"

"I'm giving you a story." Frankie rolled down the window. "Don't know why because I've never told anyone about my suspicions before. Not even Elspeth."

"I've got an honest face?"

"Everyone thinks Big Don was an out-and-out villain. I prefer to think of him as a complex man." Her eyes took on a faraway look. "He had a bad reputation but I liked him. What's more, my daughter was in love with his son."

"I think that's meant to be a secret."

"A mother always knows." Frankie winked at Dark. "Now I have to ask for that second favour."

"I'll do my best."

"Big Don was what we call in these parts a 'hard man'. His wife died when Billy was young and he had no idea how to bring up the boy or show him proper affection. He was awful hard on Bill, no doubt about it. Berated him. Belittled him."

"Charming."

"But Billy was all he had left. And despite everything, I know Don loved him. He would *never* have stopped searching for Bill."

"What are you getting at?"

"I'm saying the Laird didn't commit suicide. He simply wasn't the type. Not without knowing the truth about what happened to his kid."

"You think there was foul play?"

"I do. But the police in these parts weren't going to properly investigate the death of some smuggler, in case it came out he had them all on the take."

"And that's where I come in?"

"I've gotten nowhere, but you *claim* to be a researcher and that's the nearest I have to a detective."

Frankie fixed Dark with a piercing stare.

"Find out who killed the Laird and what happened to Billy Milne. Then you'll have a real story and I'll have closure at last."

"I'll do my utmost. I can guarantee that." Dark bit her lip. "Lachlan swears he has no clue what happened to Billy."

"I believe him."

"And all the information I have about Big Don Milne is what you and Elspeth have told me. Is there anyone else around who knew him well? Someone with a different perspective?"

"Not really. Don's old crew won't talk to you, I'm sure of that. He and Lachlan were on first-name terms but that was cause Lachie was Billy's mate. They weren't exactly friends." Frankie sighed. "The Laird didn't have any friends."

"What about enemies?"

"Plenty of them - but I can't imagine they'll invite you in for a chat."

Frankie hesitated, obviously weighing up an unpalatable idea.

"You could speak to Gordon Crabbe, Don's neighbour and the local busybody," she said slowly. "He's head of the Rotary Club and a member of the PTA, even though his daughter's 46 and lives in Glasgow."

"I know the type," Dark giggled. "Isn't that one of the names you gave me when I first turned up?"

"It was. Not much happens round here he doesn't know about and he always had a particular bee in his bonnet about Big Don."

"Any idea why?"

"Not the specifics. Most people didn't tangle with the Laird but Gordon used to come round boasting how he was going to put an end to the illegal shenanigans in Aftonhouse and asking me all sorts of questions about Don, Billy and Lachlan."

"I presume you didn't answer?"

"I eventually showed him the toe of my boot and he hasn't talked to me since. Might speak to you, though. He'd be all impressed at a big city features writer paying him attention."

"I also presume he didn't put an end to their illegal shenanigans?"

"Course not. He's just a windbag." Frankie shrugged apologetically. "It's all I got."

Dark dropped Frankie off, got out her mobile and dialled the number the woman had given her.

Gordon Crabbe here. The voice was high and lilting. *How can I help you?*

"My name is Dorothy Arrowsmith and I'm writing an article on Aftonhouse for a national magazine."

Aye. I know you are.

Of course he did. Everyone around here knew everyone else's business.

"I was wondering if you'd be willing to give me an interview."

I'm a busy man but I suppose I could spare you a few minutes.

"When might you be free?"

You can come over now. I've just finished my constitutional.

"Thank you." Dark stifled a giggle. "I've already got your address, so I'll be there in fifteen minutes."

Gordon Crabbe lived in a solidly built Victorian brick farmhouse, surrounded by a picture-perfect garden with a small orchard out back. He was standing in his doorway when Dark pulled up. Willowy, with grey mutton chops offsetting his lack of hair, he sported tweed trousers and a matching waistcoat - the epitome of a country gent.

He ushered Dark into a floral-patterned dining room and bade her sit while he fetched a decanter and two glasses. He filled them with amber liquid and sat down.

"Bit early for whisky," Dark winced.

"It's pear juice."

"That stuff's really big round here, isn't it?"

"All right, Miss Arrowsmith. If you have questions, ask away."

"I came here to write a normal tourist piece and I have." Dark had given a lot of thought on how to approach this. "But I've become rather fascinated by what might be called the… less savoury activities that went on in Aftonhouse."

"Those have been somewhat curtailed since the death of Big Don Milne. Though some other reprobate will no doubt take his place once a suitable time has elapsed." Crabbe wiped droplets from his moustache. "Lachlan Robertson would be my guess."

"Lachlan?" Dark feigned surprise. "I know he has a past but I'm told he's quite respectable these days."

"I presume he's the one who informed you of that. I believe you've been consorting with him somewhat."

"Actually, it was Frankie Cameron. She also said you knew everything that went on around here."

"I'm sure she put it in far less complimentary terms." Crabbe raised an eyebrow. "She viewed Lachlan Robertson in far too flattering a light. Big Don Milne too, for that matter."

"You're not a fan?"

"Between them, they destroyed my livelihood. And took the life of Lachlan's father, Chick Robertson."

The statement was delivered simply and without emotion. Dark was completely taken aback.

"If you're talking about the death of his wife and son, I'm assured it was an accident."

"I'm not speaking of that." Crabbe indicated the large Victorian windows allowing light to flood into the room. "Take a look out there and tell me what you see."

Dark got up and walked over. A truly beautiful vista was spread before her. A valley filled with arable land where sheep grazed on emerald fields. To her right, in the distance, she could just make out the hill where the Laird's abandoned mansion squatted. To her left, Spiral Wood was just visible on the horizon, partly obscured by haze.

"It's lovely."

"People used to call it the Golden Triangle," Crabbe said proudly. "My farm, Chick Robertson's pastures and Big Don Milne's haulage property, all bordering each other. At one time, we got on just fine. I was aware of Don's... sideline but happy to live and let live."

He fetched a pipe and a packet of tobacco from a drawer.

"Chick had a great little estate. Access to the main road and a path that led down through the cliffs to an inlet with a jetty. This is a rocky coastline and it was the only proper access to the sea for miles."

He began to pack the pipe, not looking up.

"But farming is a hard life, young lady, even if you love it - and Chick didn't. He couldn't grow fucking cacti in an oasis and was heavily in debt. I was the opposite and wanted to expand my business."

"While I'm fascinated by the logistics of agriculture, I'm not sure where you're going with this?"

"I offered to buy his land. Said he could keep living in the farmhouse free of charge. It was generous."

"Sounds fair."

"Oh, Chick was over the moon. Yet his wife, Helen, wouldn't hear of it. Then she died." Crabbe lit his pipe with a flourish. "Chick blamed Lachlan and threw him out."

"That's not fair," Dark objected.

"I didn't think so either. Not at the time." Crabbe waved a cloud of smoke away. "Father and son never got on but, in all honesty, it should have been Chick out there tending the strays. Christ, I stood at that very window and watched Lachlan materialise out of the snow, exhausted and frozen, after running through the storm for miles."

He puffed furiously, sending grey plumes into the air. Dark was too engrossed to object.

"Helen was hardly in her grave when Chick made the same deal with Big Don as he had with me. Maybe he was threatened. Maybe he was just a greedy bastard." Another cloud wafted into the air. "Either way, he didn't live long enough to enjoy the spoils. You haven't touched your juice."

Dark silently took a sip.

"Suddenly, Lachlan was back in the house, two giant new shiny sheds sprang up right next to it and Don Milne, the smuggler, had sole access to the only beach for miles."

"I already know Lachlan worked for Don when he was young." Dark's eyes were stinging now. "That's a long time ago."

"If the Laird gifted you something, you were forever in his debt." Crabbe finally knocked out his pipe. "Drive his trucks. Store his contraband. Look after his son. Whatever he wanted. Unless you did something drastic to pay him back."

"In my line of work, you learn to size people up pretty quickly." Dark scoffed. "Lachlan's a decent guy, whatever his past."

"I'm going to fetch myself a whisky, after all." Gordon Crabbe got up and went to the drinks cabinet. "Then I shall tell you a story which may well make you re-evaluate that statement."

Maclennan Cottage 2013

Gordon

---

ordon Crabbe had been to a rather splendid party.

The conversation was amiable and wide ranging which, in his opinion, was a rarity around these parts. Consequently, he had stayed rather later than intended and drank a bit more than he meant to. Gordon was not a man who flaunted the law but had no way to get home unless he drove. He decided the safest bet was to stick to the most remote back roads he knew, which was why he found himself on the B45 late at night. No police. No houses. Most importantly, no other traffic. If his car ended up in a ditch, there would be nobody else involved.

Now he was only fifteen minutes from home, close to the Maclennan property but bursting for a piss.

Gordon tried singing loudly. Gritting his teeth. Arching his back. None of it did any good. Finally, he pulled off the road. There was no way anyone else would drive past but, just in case, he switched off the engine and lights before stumbling out of the car. The moon was almost full, casting a lambent glow on the terrain. The last thing he needed was the embarrassment of being caught crouched in the wilderness with his flies undone.

He had just emptied his bladder and pulled up his zip when he heard an engine approaching. Yet he couldn't see any lights.

Gordon instinctively ducked down behind a bush. Seconds later, a shadowy leviathan trundled past.

"Good lord!"

The truck slowed down and, for a moment, Gordon thought his car had been spotted. Instead, the vehicle turned off the road in the direction of Maclennan Cottage and was quickly swallowed by darkness.

There could be only one explanation for what he had witnessed. Gordon did a little jig on the spot and promptly fell into a ditch. He didn't care.

"All this time, I've been looking in the wrong direction," he whispered to himself. "But I've got you now, Don Milne, you knuckle-dragging troglodyte."

When he reached home, Gordon was too excited to sleep. Instead, he got out a map of the area and spread it across the dining table. Three areas were already ringed in red. Don Milne's haulage huts, Lachlan Robertson's so-called workshop sheds and the inlet jetty.

These were the places Gordon had always targeted in his quest to bring the Laird to justice. The local police were in Milne's pay but he had alerted the Highlands and Islands task force a number of times. They had raided both properties, staked out the jetty and found absolutely nothing. Meanwhile the Laird's corrupt local police would shake their heads and point out that Big Don had bested Gordon in a business deal and the man was making up things in an effort to get revenge. The last time Gordon had called to request another go, he had been less than politely told to fuck off.

In the end, he had reluctantly conceded defeat. If anything, he had helped the Laird, since the authorities were now certain Milne wasn't up to anything illicit.

He groaned inwardly. Who would have suspected a nice old couple like the Maclennans of being in cahoots with a blaggard like Don Milne? Nobody. Chuckling at his own naivety, he drew a fourth symbol on the map.

Maclennan Cottage.

This time, he wouldn't call the task force with suspicions and theories. He would gather irrefutable proof of where the Laird was storing contraband and present it to the authorities himself. But how would he know when the next operation would be? Well. He saw the lorry had tuned off its headlights to avoid detection before turning onto the Maclennan property. But the driver still needed to see where he was going.

It would be on the 15th. The next full moon.

Gordon Crabbe was an avid bird watcher and owned a top-of-the-range camera with a telephoto lens. That should do the trick. It wouldn't work well enough in the dark, no matter how strong the moonlight. But he reckoned there was no way a full shipment of contraband could be loaded or unloaded and checked in the space of one night. They would still be working at dawn and Gordon would be ready.

On the night of the 15th, he filled a flask with coffee and made himself a cheese and pickle sandwich wrapped in cellophane. Ever alert, his rottweiler was waiting at the gate for him.

"Too early for walkies, Argos my friend." He rubbed the dog behind its ears, setting off a frenzy of eye-rolling and tail wagging. "I'll take you out when I come back."

At 3.00 am, he drove to the far side of the Maclellan property and hiked over the Dichty Hills. He had scoped out the area a few days before and knew precisely where he was going.

He reached an outcrop overlooking Belle and Alasdair Maclennan's barns just as dawn was breaking. The area was a frenzy of activity, men whispering to each other and hauling crates from the cavernous interior and loading them onto three waiting trucks. Gordon raised the camera to his eye, adjusted the focus and began snapping. No sign of the Maclennans - but there was no way this could be happening without the old bastards' knowledge.

However, there was Billy Milne, pulling a handcart.

"You are so up shit creek, you young scamp." Gordon took a few more pictures. "Big Don has gotten complacent. There isn't even a lookout posted."

He heard a buzzing sound above and looked up. A circular object was hovering over his head.

"What in the name of sweet baby Jesus?"

Gorden Crabbe had heard of drones but never actually seen one. They were some kind of new fad among the wealthy and he couldn't fathom why anyone would want one.

Until now.

"Fuck, fuck, fuckity, fuck." He got up and ran.

Though no longer a young man, Gordon Crabbe was strong and fit. Even so, it was four miles back to his car across rough terrain, constantly looking over his shoulder. Several times, he stumbled and fell, scraping his palms and bruising both knees. By the time he reached his car he was shaking with exhaustion and both hands trembled as he drove.

There was no sign of Argos when he got home and his heart sank. Normally, the hound would be standing on his kennel, lolling over the fence to greet his master. He hurried up the path and burst into his house, breathing heavily and clutching his sides.

Lachlan Robertson was lounging on the couch, hunting rifle balanced across one knee.

"Where the fuck is my rottweiler?" Gordon demanded.

"Gone."

"You killed my dog?" Crabbe's knees gave way and he sank into a leather armchair. "You killed Argos?"

"Argos is on his way tae an Irish trawler with a crewman who happens tae be a dog lover."

"Why? The poor wee puppy will be devastated if separated from me."

"To stop Big Don killing him," Lachlan said. "Dog doesnae deserve tae die because you did something stupid and neither do you. What the hell were you thinking, Gordon?"

"It's Mr. Crabbe. And I was thinking I'd put away a scourge on this area for good."

"All you've done is set the Laird after your blood." Lachlan held out his hand. "Give me the camera."

"I hid it." Gordon stuck out his chin defiantly. "What are you going to do now? Torture me to see where it is, then kill me? Or are you too chicken to do Big Don's dirty work?"

Despite the outward bravado, there was a tremor in his voice.

"Are you going to hand me over to him?"

"I convinced Don that a man of your standing getting found face down in the river with nae fingernails would create too much of a stink," Lachlan replied. "Told him I could handle it without violence."

"You're out of your depth, sonny." Realising he wasn't going to be fed to the fishes, Gordon had regained some of his self-confidence. "Why do you want to protect a monster like that anyway?"

"I'm doing it for Billy. You could put Big Don away for life and I wouldn't give a shit." Lachlan snapped his finger.

"But he wasnae there, you idiot. Bill was. He'll take the fall, along with Belle and Alasdair."

"They should have thought of that before they broke the law."

"Let me tell you a few reasons why we work for the Laird." Lachlan leaned forwards. "Times are hard and money tight, especially if you're old. Don's a monster, all right, but he also has rules for his operation. Nae hard drugs. Nae human trafficking."

He tapped the barrel of his rifle.

"Can you guess the main reason, though?"

Gordon shook his head.

"Because he tells us to. And you dinnae say no to Big Don."

"Then it seems we are at an impasse." Gordon got up and stretched, surreptitiously looking around for something he could use as a weapon. "I *am* saying no to Big Don and I am *not* giving up my evidence. Now, would you like a glass of whisky before you leave?"

"It's a bit early… but yes please."

Gordon fetched two glasses from the kitchen and took them to the drinks cabinet.

"You remember when I showed up at your house a decade ago?" Lachlan said suddenly. "Trying tae save my mum and brother."

"Of course I do."

"I told the police and the trauma psychologist that I collapsed when I got here and couldnae remember anything about what had happened. But it's all coming back tae me now."

"What is?" Gordon poured two shots from a crystal decanter.

"For the first time, I recall arriving at your house just before 2.30pm. But I'm pretty sure police records state you didnae call for help until just after 3.00pm.

"That's a complete fabrication!" Gordon stiffened. "You arrived right at 3.00pm and I telephoned the ambulance service as soon as I saw you."

"It's your word against mine."

"Why would anyone believe you?" His back still to Lachlan, Gordon downed one of the drinks.

"Why would I lie? You, on the other hand, hae motive. You couldnae get your hands on my dad's farm while mum was still alive, so when you saw an opportunity tae get rid of her, you took it."

Lachlan's voice was steely.

"Only, your plan went tits up when Big Don beat you to the property, so you've harassed him ever since."

"No. That's not… that's… not fair." Gordon downed the other shot. "Nobody will fall for it."

"They dinnae have tae. Helen and Archie Robertson were loved by this community. Even the suspicion that you had a hand in their deaths will be enough tae ruin you."

"Aw, Lachlan." Gordon finally turned to face him. "That's awful cold. I don't know how you're going to live with yourself after this."

"Billy Milne is my best friend." Lachlan eased himself wearily off the couch. "He's going tae stand up to his father one day, and if he ever inherits Don's empire, he'll dismantle it. I'll not see him do time because you're miffed about not getting richer."

He slung the rifle over his shoulder.

"If you ever go after the Milne family or their… employees again, I will make what I 'remember' public and nae local organisation, business or social club will touch you with a barge pole. Do you understand?"

Gordon nodded silently.

"Good." Lachlan opened the front door. "Let's go get that camera."

Dark took a deep breath.

"I think I would like a whisky now."

"I've never told anyone that story before, much less a reporter." Crabbe placed a glass in front of her. "But I thought it important for you to have a more rounded picture of who you are dealing with."

"I consider myself warned." She took a sip and wrinkled her nose. "Though you could argue Lachlan saved you and your dog from Don Milne's wrath."

"Don't try to defend him. His actions were unconscionable."

"They were," Dark agreed. "At least I know what Lachlan did to finally get out of the Laird's debt."

"Perhaps."

"What are you implying?"

"Chick. Billy. Big Don. They're all gone now." Crabbe drained his glass. "And Lachlan Robertson is still sitting pretty in his nice wee house, free of any obligations. Also, if you think about it, a so-called artist who frequently travels to Europe is the perfect cover for a smuggler."

"I'll have to mull over that speculation for a while." Dark put down the empty glass. "I do appreciate your trust, though. Naturally, I've no intention of publishing or sharing the information."

"Thank you." Gordon Crabbe escorted her to the door. A run-down wooden kennel sat in one corner of the garden.

"Oh," Dark turned back. "I do have one question."

"Anything."

"Have you ever heard of a man called Martin Cindrić?"

"No. Never."

Dark drove home and dialled Lewis. There was no answer. Nor had he replied to her last text. She sent another.

I need to talk to you!

"Men." She threw herself on the bed with an exasperated groan. No matter how nice or charming or in love with you they seemed to be, you never knew if you could really trust them."

She pulled Spiral's memento box towards her and took out a necklace. Not a cheap piece of jewellery like Nancy's. This was expensive and finely wrought.

She looked at it for a while, then fastened the chain around her neck.

Prestonfield, Edinburgh 2024

Dark and Spiral

"**T**axi's here!"

"I'm coming." Dark emerged from the bedroom.

Spiral was waiting in the lounge. He had on a pressed white shirt with a tie, black jeans and shining engineer boots. Dark had never seen him wear anything smart before.

"You are sexy as hell," she whistled. "Like Johnny Cash but a lot more handsome."

Spiral was staring at her.

"What?" She checked herself in the mirror. "You said to look my best."

Her simple bob gleamed like polished onyx. She wore a short, low-cut black velvet dress, sheer stockings and high-heeled boots.

"What?" she repeated.

"You are absolutely fucking stunning."

"Why, thank you, sir." She bowed. "Where are we going? A funeral?"

"You'll see." Spiral led her outside to the waiting cab.

"Ballroom dancing?" Dark volunteered as they climbed inside. "Millionaire Bingo? Are we joining the FBI?"

"Prestonfield House restaurant, please."

"No kidding?" Dark cried. "I've always wanted to go there."

"I know. You've told me often enough." Spiral looked down at his pristine shirt. "If I spill food on this, you'll be able to see the stain from Glasgow."

"I'll ask them to give you a spork." Dark threw her arms around Spiral. "Thank you so much!"

Prestonfield House was a 17th century manor house on the outskirts of Edinburgh, decorated by Italian artisans who had worked on the interior of Holyrood Palace.

The taxi wound through a sculptured Dutch garden studded with fountains and strutting peacocks before drawing up in front of the gigantic building. A doorman in full highland dress opened the cab, escorted them inside the neo-classical porte-cochere and took their coats.

Spiral confirmed their reservation while Dark strolled around, open-mouthed, peering into various dining areas.

The rooms were filled with tapestries and fine furnishings, many of the pieces three centuries old. They were eventually ushered into an antechamber then given nibbles and a menu.

"Would sir and madam like some champagne," the waiter inquired.

"I'll have a glass of Pinot Grigio." Spiral grinned at Dark. "I presume you don't want bubbly?"

"I'll have a Bloody Mary."

"Certainly. We have 27 different types of vodka."

Dark gave Spiral a panicked look.

"Grey Goose, please," he said. The waiter nodded sagely and drifted off.

"Thanks," Dark patted her cheeks. "I didn't want to ask for Tesco's own brand but it's the only one I know."

She fingered his tie mischievously.

"Is it wrong to want to have sex with you right now?"

"It's very right, but we're trying to appear respectable."

"I'll use these to disguise my accent." Dark stuffed a handful of candied almonds into her mouth and giggled.

After the drinks were finished, the waiter took them to their table. They were in a window corner, flanked by Chinoiserie lacquer cabinets. The walls were covered with oil paintings of serious-looking men in powdered wigs and gilded leather coverings from Cordova. Outside, they could see stables surrounded by trees, each decked with fairy lights. It was magical.

"How did you score such a nice spot on a Saturday night?" Dark whispered.

"Told them I was the son of Johnny Cash."

They ordered food and wine and joked and laughed through the entrees and main course. When the waiter had removed the plates, Spiral cleared his throat.

"I've been opaque about my past," he announced. "And you have been incredibly patient."

"Nah. I just got fed up asking."

"It's time you got some measure of truth from me," he said. "This is a kind of pre-truth dinner."

"I've no idea what that means but I'll play along."

"The first thing I have to say is that there's only one thing in this world I'm certain about. You are the love of my life." He looked faintly embarrassed. "There have been women before you…"

"A lot of women."

"You'd be surprised how few," he countered. "But there will never be anyone after this. I can guarantee it."

Dark thought she detected a note of despair in the declaration but brushed the thought away. This certainly wasn't a typical Spiral Wood diatribe.

"I love you too. Especially after bringing me here."

Spiral fished in his pocket and brought out a small velvet box.

"It's not a ring, so don't blow a gasket. But I'm coming to that."

Dark opened it. Inside was a delicate antique cameo necklace.

"This is wonderful!" She fastened it around her neck. "I'll never take it off."

"We've had a mad time," Spiral continued. "But I've begun to think properly about the future. I want to spend it with you."

"I like the way this conversation is going."

"I'm done being on the wrong side of the law and I'm happy to get a job. Ok. Not happy. But you're worth it."

"I could open a studio painting circular saws."

"Dark." Spiral took her hand. "I have one piece of unfinished business that I've got to undertake. More than that, it's a solemn promise I made to someone."

"And what's that promise?"

"Tomorrow, I have to go to the highlands for a few days. When I come back, you'll be stuck with me forever if that's what you want. Ring and everything."

"I'm certainly not averse to the idea." Dark squeezed his fingers. "Why don't I come along? I'd love to explore more of Scotland."

"No. This is something you cannot be party to."

"Why not?" She let go of his hand. "Is it dangerous? Is it illegal?"

"Both. But I have to right a terrible wrong," Spiral said evenly. "If I don't, a good friend can never be safe and neither can I."

"You're right, Spiral," Dark frowned. "I've been incredibly patient. But my tolerance is at an end. Dangerous? Illegal? That's not acceptable. Stop talking in riddles and let me know exactly what's going on."

"I'll tell you everything if I come back. Answer any question. You have to trust me. I'm begging you to trust me."

Dark's eyes widened.

"What the fuck do you mean *if* I come back?"

"*When* I come back." Spiral blanched. "I meant, when I come back."

"Where are you heading?"

"I can't say."

Dark was inclined to let it go. But if he couldn't be open now, when would it end?

"I've put up with your evasions and vagueness up till this point," she said. "I'm even willing to accept if you never tell me your history because what we have is wonderful. But it's time to draw a line in the sand."

She narrowed her eyes.

"I *will* be part of any decisions about our future. It's not negotiable. Where exactly are you going and why are you leaving me behind?"

"I can't tell you."

"Yes, you can. I'm your partner."

"No."

The single word was delivered with such coldness it was like a slap in the face. Suddenly, all of Dark's frustrations bubbled to the surface.

"I refuse to live on the outskirts of your life anymore. Tell me, Spiral!"

"You'd try to talk me out of it and it's something I have to do."

"Stop making assumptions." Dark unfastened her necklace and put it on the table. "I can't be with someone who won't share something this important."

"You have to trust me," he repeated.

"You obviously don't trust *me*."

"Please, Dark." Spiral's eyes misted. "It's not like that. I'm doing it for us."

"You've no right to do anything for us without letting me in on it. That's insulting and selfish."

"True. But I simply can't go into more details."

"Yes. You can."

"You're absolutely right." Spiral closed his eyes. "However, I won't."

"*What?*"

"I won't," he repeated. "I'm not asking your permission, Dark. It's a done deal."

"You can't treat me this way. Not if you love me." She took a deep breath and clenched her fists. "Let me in or I leave right now."

"I do love you. But nothing can stop me. It's too important."

Tears glistened in Dark's eyes, but she was determined. So, she called his bluff.

"Your choice. Goodbye, Spiral."

Dark got up and left. She walked slowly, hoping with all her heart he would call out or come after her.

He didn't.

She got a taxi to a friend's flat and spent the night there. When she returned to the house next day, Spiral Wood was gone.

Dark waited for two weeks. There was no phone call. No email. She reached out to Lewis but he hadn't heard from Spiral either. Surely, he was coming back like he promised? He had left everything here, even his phone. Presumably so nobody could track him.

It was obvious he was determined not to be found.

Dark considered alerting the police but decided against it. No point in the cops hunting him down, then putting two and two together and arresting all three of them for their previous crimes.

She searched the flat for hints of what he had been up to or where he had gone, yet found nothing. Spiral had left his laptop too - but she didn't know the password and his memento box yielded no clues.

Dark drifted listlessly through the motions of normalcy. She didn't need a job. They had plenty of money. Spiral had left her details of his bank account and though she checked frequently, he never withdrew any cash.

She wondered if he was dead. Scoured the newspapers. Checked again with Lewis.

Nothing.

One night, she took Spiral's favourite novel, *The Great Gatsby*, off the bookshelf and curled up with it in a chair. When she opened the cover, a photograph fell out. Spiral must have hidden it there, believing she would never get around to reading it. It showed a young boy standing outside a place called Aftonhouse Post Office.

Dark picked it up and studied the picture. It looked a lot like Spiral, though she couldn't be certain. Had he been using it as a bookmark or was it some sort of clue? The former was more likely but the latter gave her the strength to try and find out.

She looked around the flat. Empty wine bottles littered every surface, wastebaskets overflowed, clothes were strewn across the floor and the sink was piled high with dishes.

She decided to pull herself together, clean up the flat and use it as an excuse to have one more search. She dusted, washed, hoovered and tidied the place from top to bottom.

Under Spiral's desk was a paper shredder. Dark took off the top and was about to empty it into a bin bag when she stopped.

Why not? She had nothing better to do.

She emptied the shredder onto the pine floor instead. Then she fetched a tea tray and Scotch tape.

For two days, she sifted and sorted through the strips of paper and card, painstakingly piecing them together.

When she was finally done, she looked at the results in horror.

Then she packed a suitcase and Googled the location of Aftonhouse.

She packed a suitcase, rented a car and drove north.

Cameron's Store 2024

Dark and Frankie

Dark got up at dawn, brewed coffee and made her daily pilgrimage to the memento box. She removed some shredded printouts held together by multiple strips of clear tape.

One was a scanned letter, printed and heavily annotated with Spiral's handwriting. It looked like a rough draft but, instead of creating a clearer message, the corrections seemed designed to have the opposite effect. Now, it looked like it was written by someone lacking in finesse and education. Words had been deliberately altered to be misspelt and the punctuation was clumsy.

Scrawled across the top in red pen were the words **Last Ever Con**.

To Martin Cindrić

I bet you have been looking for your wife and by now you must be thinking that she is not so easy to find, eh? I am shure you probably questioned Big Don Milne before you killed him and faked his suicide. But you did not find what you wanted, because he was double-crossed too.

The attached pictures should be proof that I am not pretending. Your wife looks like she's enjoying herself, eh? This is the man who is with her. He thinks you have given up looking for him but I bet he is wrong.

In four days at 6.00am I will be at the same place where the last exchange was supposed to happen. I want one million pounds in used notes, delivered personally by you. This is because you will be sending your men to Dundee, where your wife now lives. I know what you look like and I will not come near unless you are alone.

You will give me the money and I will tell you exactly where your wife and her lover live. This will give your men time to check that I am telling the truth. Then I will leave with the cash.

If you do not personally show up on your own, I will tell your wife you are still searching and she will go on the run once more. You will never hear from me again and she can live a happy life with her new mister.

The second and third printouts were blown-up photographs.

One showed a naked woman lying seductively on a couch in Lachlan Robertson's house. In the second, Lachlan and the same woman had their arms around each other, smiling into the camera. Dark had never seen her in real life but she'd recognised the face immediately.

It was the girl in the painting hanging on Spiral Wood's wall.

Dark still had no idea who Martin Cindrić was. Didn't have all the pieces to put the puzzle together. Yet she knew who did. She'd figured that out some time ago and wasn't going to be put off anymore.

She got out her mobile and dialled.

Is that you, Dark? A sleepy voice answered. *You know what time of the morning it is?*

"You're going to drive up here today, Lew," Dark said. "I have a spare room where you can stay the night and I'll see you in the morning."

Why would I do that?

"To tell me about Spiral's last ever con. The one involving Martin Cindrić."

There was silence for a long time.

You know a lot more than you've been letting on, don't you?

"I'm still working it out." Dark's voice hardened. "But I've learned enough to know you've been lying through your teeth about everything."

It never sat well with me, Lewis finally admitted. *But Spiral and I both thought we were doing the right thing.*

"And my feelings don't count?"

Your feelings were the only thing Spiral ever cared about.

There was another long pause.

I'll be there. Text me directions.

"The key will be under the mat. Don't go through the village or let anyone see you."

I know that tone of voice, Lewis said. *You're pulling a con, too.*

"Just get here, Lew. Or else."

Dark hung up.

She drove to Aftonhouse and parked outside Cameron's grocery store.

"Hi, Dark." Elspeth was seated behind the counter, as always.

"Is your mum upstairs?"

"She is. Go on through if you like."

"Thanks."

Dark sprinted up the stairs and knocked on the door. Frankie opened it, still wearing her nightdress.

"Oh!" She ushered Dark in. "I'm not decent."

"I'll make some coffee while you get dressed."

"All right." The woman disappeared into the bedroom. When she emerged, two mugs were on the breakfast bar.

"I didn't expect another visit so soon." She sat on a stool and sipped her drink. "How can I help you?"

"I've got a few more questions, if you don't mind."

"I presume this isn't about the article," Frankie said. "On the case already, eh?"

"I spoke to Gordon Crabb. He had some interesting theories about Lachlan Robertson and Billy Milne."

"Painted a rather unflattering picture of them, I imagine." Frankie sniffed disdainfully. "You should talk to Lachie about him rather than me."

"Gordon suggested Lachlan might not be an entirely reliable source."

"We all have our own take on people and events," Frankie said guardedly. "There are certain things *I* have no wish to revisit."

"You will if you want to know what really happened to the Laird." Dark hesitated. "Were you two an item?"

"We were closer than most people knew," Frankie replied evasively. "After my husband died, he was good to me."

"Gossip is, Bill helped himself to the contents of his dad's safe right before he vanished. You think it's possible?"

"I don't listen to local chatter."

"This came from Elspeth. And I'm pretty sure Big Don would have confided in you."

"*Someone* absconded with Don's money." Frankie pulled a face. "If it was Billy, that was a low blow, in my opinion. Big Don still left everything to him in his will."

"Don didn't really think Billy was dead, then?"

"Perhaps it was easier than accepting his only son had robbed him and taken off."

"Lachlan left at exactly the same time. Pretty big coincidence."

"Lachie said he went on a gallery tour of Europe and I've no reason to doubt it."

"I'm not out to cause trouble for either of them," Dark reassured her. "Just doing what you asked."

"I realise that, dear. I'm simply not sure where you're going with this."

"You talked about an accident involving Lachlan's mum and brother," Dark ploughed on. "Elspeth didn't seem keen on you elaborating about it."

"And she was right. It's Lachlan's affair."

"He already told me the details. I want to know more about how it *affected* him."

"I'll make toast." Frankie got up. "Listen. Do you really care about Lachie?"

"I do."

"All right," The woman put two slices of bread in the toaster. "He made the right decision, leaving Helen and Archie to try and get help. Still, his father couldn't forgive him. I took Lachie in but the whole sorry affair had messed with his head. He became bitter. Distant. Unsatisfied. Started doing dodgy jobs for Big Don."

Her voice was laden with regret.

"In a way, he began to rival Billy in the Laird's affections. Because Lachie took on the risky stuff, Bill became less involved in the operation. Eventually, he was reduced to being little more than a gofer."

The bread popped up and Frankie began to spread butter on the slices.

"Did Billy resent that?"

"We talked about it once, right at this table. Do you know what Bill told me?" When she put the toast on the table, there were tears in Frankie's eyes. "He said Lachie was his best friend and that was all there was to it. That Lachlan was trying to help him."

She gave an unhappy laugh.

"When his dad suddenly died, Lachie moved back into the farmhouse, sorted himself out and I rarely saw him after that."

Dark squinted at her companion. She had a con artist's instincts for when people were lying and knew Frankie was being evasive.

"Bitter. Distant. Unsatisfied." Dark got up and strode to the window. Looked out at the hills, trying to regain her composure. "Do you think he's really changed?"

"I do," Frankie replied vehemently. "And I resent the tack you're taking, young lady."

"You've never known him to be violent?"

Frankie was quiet for a while.

"He saw Elspeth being harassed by a couple of local lads once," she said. "He respectfully asked them to leave her alone. When they carried on, he knocked them both out."

"I'd say that was pretty…"

"Then he drove them to a local doctor to make sure they were OK."

"Oh."

"If you think Lachie had anything to do with Billy's disappearance or Don's death, you're barking up the wrong tree." Frankie pushed the plate away, untouched "Why are you pursuing this line? I think you owe me that much."

"It's been my experience that we don't know the people we love as much as we think." Dark took the less explicit printed picture from her bag and handed it to Frankie. "Recognise this woman?"

"That's Eva Stone. She cleaned house for the Laird now and then." Frankie seemed surprised. "Looks like she and Lachie were an item. I didn't know that."

She traced wrinkled fingers over the sellotaped lines.

"Why was it shredded? You're not going all psycho and stalkerish, are you?"

"I didn't do it," Dark assured her. "I heard she left Aftonhouse around the same time as Billy."

"Yeah. Big Don told me he had to let her go, what with his money getting pinched. He was sure it wasn't her doing - but few of the other households would have kept her on, just in case. Said he gave her a couple of weeks wages with the train fare to Edinburgh and a recommendation."

This time, Frankie was telling the truth.

"What's going on?" the woman pressed. "What's Ewa got to do with all this?"

"Please bear with me." Dark put the picture away. "I am totally on Lachlan's side, but I need to know one more thing."

"All right," she said uneasily. "Carry on."

"Did anyone in Aftonhouse actually see Eva leave?"

"Not that I'm aware of." Frankie pushed back her chair and emptied the toast into the bin. "What's going on, Dark? I wanted answers, not more questions."

"I can't tell you just yet," Dark replied. "I'm asking you to trust me."

She was all too aware Spiral Wood had begged for the very same thing. Instead of acquiescing, she had stormed out of the restaurant and left him on his own.

"I not sure that I do. Not if you're hiding things from me."

Dark's lips tightened.

"That works both ways, Frankie."

"You're always welcome here but I think I've said enough. Lachlan Robertson is a wonderful man. Period."

"I owe you my thanks and a proper explanation." Dark stood up. "You have the first, and you'll get the second as soon as I'm able. And I'll still put up Elspeth in Edinburgh."

"Hmmm." The woman grunted. "I'm not so sure that's a good idea anymore."

"I understand that you're angry with my evasiveness," Dark said sadly. "But now *I* have to right a terrible wrong."

She went downstairs. Elspeth looked up from her magazine.

"That was quick. Is everything all right?"

"Not in the slightest. I'll be back when it is."

Dark got into her car and looked at her watch. 9.00 am.

She switched on the engine and began to text.

Robertson Farm 2024

Dark and Lachlan

Lachlan got up, dressed and switched on his mobile. There was a message from Dark.

Finally finished my article. Be coming round about 10.00 am.

He glanced at the clock.

"Plenty of time." He strolled downstairs and made coffee and cereal. Outside, the sky was overcast and threatening rain. He was about to carry breakfast to the table when the phone rang.

As he bent to pick it up, the window cracked and a plate on the shelf behind him exploded. He threw himself to the floor as another bullet punctured the glass and embedded itself in the wall.

He pulled the phone over and pressed receive.

"Almost there!" Dark shouted cheerfully, "Feel free to be naked."

"Dark, listen! Don't come here…"

But she had hung up.

Lachlan crawled across the room, through the open door, and scooted up the stairs to the hall cupboard. He raced back down, rifle in hand, threw open the front door and darted out. Within seconds he had reached the wheelbarrow and hunkered behind it.

Nothing.

He slid onto his belly and scanned the area through his telescopic sight.

Nobody.

Lachlan glanced over his shoulder at the window. There were two deformed gaps, surrounded by a spider web of cracks. Not a shotgun, then. Probably not a rifle either - that would have left a neat hole. Most likely a handgun, which meant the assailant had to have been relatively close, perhaps shooting from the road. Lachlan hadn't heard a car or motorbike. Then again, he wasn't listening. Or the would-be assassin had fled on foot in any one of a dozen directions.

Now he could make out the sound of an engine now, growing louder.

"Aw shit."

Dark's rental car hove into view over the rise and stopped outside his gate.

Without a second thought, Lachlan stood up and gestured for her to stay in the vehicle.

Dark got out and waved back.

"Nice to see you too!" she shouted. "Why are you carrying your rifle?"

Her eyes widened as Lachlan sprinted towards the car, grabbed her waist and forced her to the ground.

"Someone just tried tae kill me." He pointed at the window.

"Holy Christ." Her face changed to a look of panic. "Is he still here?"

"I dinnae think so." He pulled her up and jogged back to the front door, shielding her body with his own. He hustled her upstairs and into his bedroom, where any aggressor would be unable to see them.

"You spot any other vehicles on your way here?"

"No." Dark rubbed her arm where she had landed on the tarmac. "You have to call the police!"

"Nae point," Lachlan said calmly. "Whoever did this will be long gone by the time they arrive and, anyway, the local cops are useless and no too fond of me."

He grimaced sourly.

"What I need tae call is a glazier. It'll be freezing in that kitchen tonight."

"Good God. Does nothing ever faze you?"

"Well, I dinnae like being cold."

"Who the hell would shoot at you? Is it the guy I saw outside your balcony that time?"

"Beats me." He squinted at her. "Any chance your ex-boyfriend has suddenly reappeared?"

"If he did, he'd use charisma to try and win me back, not a bloody firearm." Dark glanced nervously around. "I'm scared, Lachlan."

"I've been alerted now and have a much better weapon, so whoever it was will be heading for the hills. I doubt we're in any immediate danger."

"Should we go to my place, just in case?"

"That's just as isolated." Lachlan stroked his chin. "Let's check into Aftonhouse Hotel until we decide what to do. You stay here and I'll pack a bag. The village isn't exactly a metropolis, but there are too many people around for a repeat performance of this little stunt. And the locals can sniff out a stranger with their eyes closed."

"Can I get clothes from my house, at least?"

"I've still got some stuff that belonged tae Ewa Jakubowicz in my wardrobe. Or is that too weird?"

"It's turning out to be a strange day. I'll roll with it."

"We'll be safe, I promise." He kissed her trembling hand. "And the restaurant is nice, as you know."

"All right. Take your gun, though. And we'll be running for the car."

"Ladies first."

"This was quite a shock." Dark kissed him back. "But I can't deny it was exciting. It's made me a bit horny."

"I thought you were terrified."

"I was. But now I have a macho highlander with a cannon to protect me," she smirked. "Don't suppose you have a kilt you could throw on?"

"It's getting dry cleaned." Lachlan laughed with her. "Anyway, if we're sharing a hotel room, there's no way I'm risking getting shot in the knacks."

The elderly hotel receptionist looked astonished at actually having guests.

"Name?" She opened the register.

"Mr. and Mrs. Smith," Dark replied with a smirk. "I've always wanted to say that."

The woman didn't smile.

"Sorry, I may be slightly hysterical."

"It's me, Alison," Lachlan sighed. "Lachlan Robertson. And this is Dark Arrowsmith."

"I ken aw that, but I'm supposed tae ask." The woman peered over her glasses. "Do ye need help with your bags? Or that rifle?"

"Dark's a big game hunter." Lachlan handed his companion the gun. "I'm just showing her around while my windows are being replaced. I'll bring the bags later."

Alison accepted this without a change of expression.

"Can I make a dinner reservation for 8.00 pm? And has anyone seen a stranger in the village the last couple of days?"

"Yes tae the first. No tae the second."

"Would you let me ken if you do?"

"Not that I'm the local gossip but of course I will." She handed him a key and a smile finally cracked her face.

"Honeymoon suite. Top floor."

Once they were in the room, they almost tore each other's clothes off and made love with a strange mixture of tenderness and passion. Afterwards, they lay in each other's arms, bathed in sweat.

"What are we going to do about your mysterious enemy?" Dark asked. "If you're determined not to get the police involved."

"I dinnae hae a lot of choices." Lachlan caressed her hair. "I'll wait for him tae make another move and hope I anticipate it in time."

"*That's* your plan?"

"When you spent a good bit of your youth working with the son of the local villain, you got used tae looking over your shoulder."

"Except, this time, you can't call Bill for backup."

"I can handle things on my own." Lachlan yawned. "Let's hae a sleep, then go tae dinner. Trying to stay alive has made me pretty hungry. Plus the sex, of course."

Dark and Lachlan sat next to each other in a quiet restaurant booth, sipping wine. Both faced the door, just in case.

Dark was wearing a bright red dress that belonged to Ewa. It made her feel more of an imposter than ever.

"I wish they'd let me bring my rifle," Lachlan grunted. "Apparently, it's not good dining etiquette."

"Don't sweat it." Dark picked up a serrated knife. "This is why I ordered steak."

She put a hand to her mouth.

"I forgot you were a vegetarian."

"But not a food Nazi. Eat what you like."

"You risked your life for me today," Dark said. "I don't know how even to begin processing that. Or how to thank you."

"I'm Scottish. Pay for dinner and we're even."

"We've been dancing around each other, Lachlan." She scratched her temple. "I've got so many secrets and I don't know how to share them."

"I like you fine the way you are." Lachlan patted her hand. "Just dinnae mistake my acquiescence for lack of interest. I'm dying tae know more about you but it's your choice."

He took a huge gulp of wine.

"God, I'll miss you when you go back to Edinburgh."

"I'm no longer sure I want to." Dark couldn't look him in the eye. "Not after meeting you. That wasn't supposed to happen."

"Are we finally sharing?" There was a twinkle in his eye. "That frightens me mair than any gunman."

Dark's heart was racing. She wanted desperately to tell Lachlan everything and knew it was impossible. In a day or so, yes. Not now. Not till things played out.

And yet… He deserved *something*.

She took a deep breath.

"I didn't come up here to write an article on Aftonhouse," she blurted out.

"I ken. That's why I was so quick tae get chummy."

"*What?*" Dark's heart sank.

"Dinnae fret. My feelings for you have turned very genuine."

"I mean, *how* did you know?"

"Frankie Cameron is a wise old bird." Lachlan gave a lopsided grin. "She phoned *Scots Magazine* to check your credentials."

"Oh." Dark closed her eyes.

"They had nae idea who you were."

"I...eh…" she stammered. "Aw, fuck."

She had wanted to come clean and now her hand was forced. Oddly, all she felt was a sense of relief.

"I'm a confidence trickster," she said simply.

"Is that so?" Lachlan's eyebrows shot up. "Are you here to diddle me?"

To Dark's astonishment, he grinned broadly.

"I might hae phrased that a bit better."

"I came here looking for my ex. That much is true. He was a con man too - and I'm pretty certain he was up here to pull one last job. A job I don't know anything about. He never came back, so I went searching for the truth."

"You couldnae just admit that tae begin with?"

"Doesn't exactly engender faith in me, does it?"

"I trust you," Lachlan said. "Why not?"

"You are fucking impossible!" Dark pointed her fork at him. "You should hate me."

"I should. But I'm nuts about you." Lachlan batted the implement away. "What's a guy tae do?"

Dark stared.

"I'd had the crazy idea coming here would lead me to my ex," she said finally. "I'd figured out he grew up in this area."

"Tell me his name, then. I might even have known him."

"He called himself Spiral Wood. Fake, of course, but you see what I'm getting at."

"The place where I happen to live. Intriguing." Lachlan rubbed his hands together. "So you put two and two together."

"And got five," Dark said dolefully. "Instead of answers, I found more mysteries. And you."

"That a bad thing?"

"Yes," she replied emphatically. "I'm not exactly in the right headspace to fall for some mysterious highlander. But I have. Hard."

"Which is what a con woman *would* say. Are these added mysteries the reason someone is trying to shoot me?"

Dark burst into tears.

"This is *so* fucked! I want you. I loved him. I still don't know what crazy stunt he was trying to pull but I can't move on until I find out what happened."

"Hey." Lachlan pulled her close. "We'll work it out. But I notice you evaded the question about me getting killed."

"I think *I* might be the real target. Perhaps I'm getting too close to the answers."

"And those answers involve Billy Milne, the Laird dying, Ewa and some guy called Martin Cindrić?"

Dark's eyes widened at the name.

"You've had quite a chat with Frankie, eh?"

"I have. I've also never heard of any Martin Cindrić."

"Neither has anyone else around here. However, Cindrić is definitely the missing piece of this puzzle."

"Then you'll be staying with me for the next few days until you suss it out. All right?"

"I'd like that a great deal. But I have a friend of Spiral's called Lewis coming up tomorrow and I reckon he can shed light on the whole thing."

"Then we'll say no more about it for now." Lachlan kissed her. "Let's enjoy our dinner and we can get dessert tae go."

Dark and Lachlan lay in bed, holding each other.

"For a town where nothing much happens," Dark said. "This is turning out to be quite an electrifying place."

"I've been giving a lot of thought tae what you told me." Lachlan gently stroked her hair.

"About being a confidence trickster? Or about me wanting you?"

"That is most certainly in the forefront of my mind. But also this mysterious Martin Cindrić." He propped himself up on one elbow. "As I say, I dinnae ken who he is, but I can make a shrewd guess."

"Really?"

"She refused to talk about him," Lachlan said. "However, I'm pretty sure he was Ewa Jakubowicz's husband."

"Tell me." Dark laid her head on his shoulder. "Tell me everything."

All right." Lachlan said. "It all started on one of my trips to Europe."

Stockholm 2021

Lachlan and Ewa

Lachlan sat on a pale blue leather bench in the Moderna Museet in Stockholm. This early in the morning, the place was almost deserted. A guard looked in, gave him a brief nod and vanished again.

The gallery had recently bought one of his pieces and he had helped bring in and install the sculpture. Nobody knew Lachlan was the creator, assuming he was simply a workman sent over to help with the heavy lifting. That was another reason he liked to stay anonymous. He couldn't deny he got a thrill seeing his work in such auspicious surroundings. Still, he didn't want to be treated differently from any other visitor.

Besides, *this* was the real reason he was here.

Two sheets of glass stood in front of him, divided by a line and filled with mysterious symbols. It resembled some window propped up on a table.

Lachlan got up, walked around it and sat down again, a contented smile on his face.

A woman entered, accompanied by two men. Lachlan watched them with detached curiosity. The female was tall and slim, expensively dressed in a red velvet coat. Her wavy blond hair was cut in a severe fringe at the front, long at the sides, the perfect frame for an innocent face and high cheekbones. She was as stunning as any painting.

The men accompanying her were both burly, with shaved heads and green puffer jackets. One had an ugly scar running down the side of his face. They paid no attention to the artwork on the walls but kept a close eye on the woman. Bodyguards of some sort, Lachlan assumed, judging by their lack of enthusiasm for the wonders on display.

To his surprise, the woman came and sat next to him, a little too close for social convention.

Must be a European thing, he thought.

One of the men stayed at the entrance. The other stood in front of Lachlan, hands on hips, expecting him to move.

"Sorry, pal," Lachlan said pleasantly. "I cannae see the sculpture."

The man looked perturbed. He was an intimidating presence and clearly not used to being dismissed. The woman opened a gallery guide, a small smile on her face.

"I think it is you who should move," he replied menacingly.

"You got a wee bit of fluff stuck there." Lachlan reached forwards and ran a hand down the stranger's crotch. He leapt back, surprise turning to fury.

"That's better," Lachlan grinned. "Dinnae knock over the sculpture, though. Not unless you brought a lot of pocket money."

The woman's smile widened and she quickly hid it behind the pamphlet.

The man took a step towards him.

"What I'm saying is," Lachlan continued evenly. "This is *not* a place you want tae start a fight. Especially no with me."

He turned to the woman and pointed to the sculpture.

"That's one of the few replicas of *The Bride Stripped Bare by Her Suitors, Even,* sanctioned by its artist, Marcel Duchamp."

"It has meaning for you?" The woman's accent was crisply clipped, like her companion. Polish, he guessed. "Perhaps you could explain."

"I could. How bored would you like tae be?"

"I cannot get more bored." She glanced towards the thug, who was still glaring at Lachlan.

"Everyone has their interpretation of what it means," Lachlan said. "From the frustrations of love and sex tae the physics of electromagnetism and the fourth dimension."

"It looks like a window."

"It kind of is, really. The Bride's that bug-like thing at the top. The Bachelors are the nine anthropomorphic cylinders at the bottom. Each Bachelor is trying tae win her affection, but they exist in a completely different zone and are having a hard time communicating with her."

"I know the feeling," the woman laughed, extending a hand. "My name is Ewa, incidentally."

"Lachlan." He shook it firmly. "If you look closely, you can see nine small holes on the right side of the Bride, which Duchamp marked by firing matches with paint on the tips through a toy cannon. Unfortunately, the shots never came close tae their target. So, the Bachelors cannae reach the Bride and their love for her remains unfulfilled."

"I am starting to like Mr. Duchamp," Ewa said.

"The Bride's form resembles an antenna so she can send and receive messages. The Bachelors are not so advanced. Their only response comes in the form of those failed shots fae the toy canon, a rudimentary and pathetic means of winning her love."

"And the crack in the glass at the top?"

"One of the installers dropped it by mistake. Apparently, Duchamp was delighted, declaring it was finally finished."

Having failed miserably to frighten Lachlan, the bodyguard moved off. The stranger might be tough but his droning on about art was too tedious to bear. He sat next to his companion and both began to play games on their mobiles.

"I understand it better now." Ewa put down the guide. "Though the whole thing is a little abstract for me. Why do you like it so much?"

"I know something most people don't."

"Tell me."

"Marcel Duchamp had an affair with a Brazilian sculptress named Maria Martins - the love of his life. But she was married and, eventually, her husband took her back to Brazil."

"Go on."

"When the original was installed in the Philadelphia Museum of Art, Duchamp insisted they knock an actual window through tae the garden outside. The curators assumed it was intended to bathe the sculpture in natural light and he was being a diva."

Lachlan lowered his voice.

"They didnae realise the window looked directly onto a sculpture in the garden. It was by Maria Martins."

Ewa's eyebrows shot up.

"This is one of the most famous and debated artworks of all time," he continued. "But, in reality, it's simply a con. Its true purpose was to have people look straight through it, tae the work of the woman Duchamp adored."

"I would love to see that."

"You can't, I'm afraid. Because Duchamp never told anyone, the sculpture was removed and the window blocked up again after he died."

"This is a beautiful and sad story." A tear slid down Ewa's cheek. "Thank you for sharing it with me."

"Hmmm." Lachlan glanced at the two men. "They're not just bodyguards, are they?"

"They work for my husband, not me. He is on business here."

"And you cannae get rid of them."

"No. But I can make them suffer by bringing them to places like this."

"Your husband won't come with you? Or am I being too forward?"

"I would not wish him to." She glanced around nervously. "He has enough treasures of his own and no inclination to share them. He prefers to keep his... possessions under lock and key."

"Including you, I assume."

"You are a perceptive man." She lifted a listless hand and let it drop again. "I am sorry. My troubles are my own and should stay that way."

Her sorrow was all too apparent. Lachlan stared at her for a long time. Made a decision.

"Suppose I were to tell you I could get you out of here?"

"My husband's men have my passport, credit cards and identification." She smiled gently at him. "I appreciate your concern, but there is nothing you can do."

"I meant, away fae *him*."

"That is very presumptuous." She made as if to rise. "I have stated no such desire."

"Then, I apologise," Lachlan shrugged. "It's just that I believe in seizing the moment when it arises."

He gave a roguish grin.

"Also, I'm pretty tight with a smuggler."

Ewa sat down again.

"What are you proposing?"

"It's less than a day's drive to Haugesund on the Norwegian coast. I call now and he'd hae a boat waiting by the time we arrived."

"Going where?"

"Scotland. Once we're there, I can get you a new identity." He gave her a winning smile. "I'm an honest man, myself, but I do know some… interesting people."

"This is an insane conversation. We have just met." Yet, a glimmer of hope sparked in Ewa's eyes.

"If I was someone you were familiar with, we'd never be able tae pull this off."

"Why would you risk your life to help a stranger?"

"Would I be risking my life?"

"Most certainly. My husband is an extremely dangerous man and everyone fears him, including me." Ewa lowered her eyes. "I cannot accept your help."

"A long time ago, I ran out on two people who were in trouble," Lachlan said. "They died and I've never forgiven myself."

"You have a guilt complex?"

"The size of Alaska. Does it matter?" He nodded towards the bodyguards. "Anyway, those guys pissed me off. And you dinnae piss a Scotsman off."

"They have *guns*, Lachlan. They've hurt people."

"Aye. I figured that out already."

"And my husband is… He's…"

"Someone you can't bring yourself to talk about." Lachlan sat up straight. "Me? I'm not looking for money, sexual favours or even gratitude. I just want tae help."

"I have tried to leave before. He always finds me."

"Not this time. Now, look intae my eyes and tell me yes or no."

She held his gaze. Took a deep breath.

"Fuck, yes."

"There's a small door in the next room," Lachlan said. "Go through it and you'll find a corridor they use to move the artworks. They all have hidden tags and there are sensors which will go off if you've stolen one, so dinnae nick a painting on your way."

"This has never occurred to me."

"Then you'll be fine. It's not staffed. Follow the corridor past the loading bay. At the end are two sets of stairs. Take the left, up one flight and you'll see a fire exit. Go out there and there's a taxi rank across the street."

"How do you know all this? Are you an international art thief?"

"I live on a farm." Lachlan grinned. "Do you have any jewellery given tae you by your husband?"

"This brooch." She tapped a chunky enamel shield embossed with gold lions pinned to her lapel. "It's my husband's family crest. Too large and gauche for my taste but he forbids me to take it off."

"That's probably because there's a small tracker inside. I imagine it's how he finds you."

"Bastard." Ewa nose wrinkled in anger.

"Hail a taxi." Lachlan passed her a 500 Krona note. "Give him this, along with your coat, bag and shoes."

"What?"

"Just in case there's more than one bug. Tell him tae take your stuff to the train station and hand it to lost property."

"He will do that?"

"For 500 Krona, he'd probably drive it to Denmark."

"And then?"

"Wait. I'll be along in ten minutes once I've taken care of your friends."

He removed a chocolate bar from his pocket, unwrapped it and nibbled the edge.

"Want some?"

"My husband likes me to stay slim."

"Take off the brooch and put it on the seat," he whispered. "Hide the movement with your guidebook."

"It is worth a fortune!"

"Is it worth your freedom? I'm asking you tae trust me."

"Strangely, I do." She unclipped the ornament and placed it on the leather. With a deft movement, Lachlan scooped up the brooch and replaced it with the chocolate bar.

"You can eat what you like once this is over."

He stood up and inspected the sculpture, keeping his body between Ewa and her minders. He enveloped the brooch in silver foil, crushed it to the same shape and pinned it inside his wallet.

"It was a pleasure meeting you, miss." He bent over and kissed her hand.

"Come for me, Lachlan. I could not bear another disappointment."

"You have my word. Go on the signal."

"What signal?"

"I think you'll know. Dinnae judge me, though."

"What do you mean?"

"I despise violence. However, I abhor ignoring injustice even more."

Lachlan got up and walked past the two thugs. He did not like what he was about to do but had no other option.

He stopped and came back.

"Excuse me," he asked. "Would you happen tae ken where the toilet is?"

One man looked up from his phone.

"Fuck off."

Lachlan shot out both arms, grabbed their heads and slammed them together. Before they could recover, he stepped back and rammed straight fingers into their sternums. The men doubled over, gasping for breath. Lachlan brought an elbow down on each thick neck at the base of the skull. They slid to the floor, unconscious.

When he looked back, Ewa had gone.

He removed the guns from their waistbands and placed them on the floor. Then he took their mobiles.

A guard skidded into the room, alerted by the noise and goggled at the carnage.

"Inspector Archer of Scotland Yard," Lachlan snapped. He opened his wallet and briefly flashed the silver wrapped brooch, tucking it away before the guard could get a proper look. "I'm assisting the Polismyndigheten, investigating a series of art thefts. I've apprehended these two in the act, but I suspect there is another heading for a getaway car."

The man stared at the pistols and swallowed hard.

"I'm going after him. Alert the authorities. Ask for Rikspolischef Elsa Bergendahl and appraise her of the situation. Oh. And call an ambulance for these two. They're just stunned but best to be on the safe side."

"Will do." The guard gave an enthusiastic salute. "You can count on me, sir."

"Good man." Lachlan sprinted away, profoundly glad he had watched so many Swedish police procedurals on Netflix. There was no Rikspolischef Elsa Bergendahl but the guard had no way of knowing that. When he got outside, he unfastened the brooch and dropped it in the nearest bin, along with the phones. Then he made for his rented car.

Ewa drove towards Haugesund, while Lachlan got out his mobile and dialled.

Hello Lachie, a highland voice answered. *I thought you were in Sweden.*

"I am, Don. But I've run intae a bit of trouble."

There was a pause.

What dae you need?

"A boat waiting at Haugesund to take me and one other back to Scotland as soon as possible. I'll also need a fake ID for a young woman."

That's a fairly big ask.

"It's an emergency."

Another pause.

Midnight. The Polar Star at dock four. You're not there? It goes anyway.

"Thank you, Don."

I owe you. And I wouldnae leave Billy's best mate in the lurch.

There was a click as the person at the other end hung up.

"That's it?" Ewa glanced at him.

"Big Don may be a villain but he's a man of his word and doesnae ask questions."

"Is this a Scottish thing?"

"Sort of." Lachlan scratched his lip. "I sense you're used tae the good life and that's not what awaits you. I hae a cottage on my property you can stay in but it's nothing special. I'll give you a cash stake tae get started but you'll probably have tae get a job."

"I am happy to be a cleaner. Freedom is riches enough."

"I dinnae want tae know your past and I'll never question you about it - not even your husband's name. You are a new person. Deal?"

"I have no desire to speak of my former life. Thank you, Lachlan. From the bottom of my heart."

Ewa reached out and took his hand.

"Where exactly are we going?"

"The arse end of nowhere," Lachlan replied. "A place called Aftonhouse."

Robertson Farm 2023

Lachlan and Ewa

Lachlan was relaxing with a glass of wine when Ewa walked in. She wasn't the type to knock.

"Are you well, Lachlan?" She never called him Lachie either.

"I'm fine. How's the house?"

He had found her a small cottage on the other side of the hill and helped her move in and decorate it.

"It is lovely."

"And the job?"

"Satisfactory."

True to his word, Big Don had given her new papers and hired her as a cleaner. She was now Eva Stone. She never talked about her past life or her former husband and Lachlan respected that.

Ewa went into the kitchen and helped herself to a glass. Pouring herself wine, she perched on the edge of the couch.

"I have a favour to ask."

"Certainly."

"I want you to do a sculpture of me. To use in any way you see fit."

"Oh." Lachlan looked awkward. "That's not really my thing. I'm nae classicist. Besides, you're trying tae keep a low profile."

"As are you, my friend. Though, if I had your talent, I would shout it from the rooftops."

Unlike most people in Aftonhouse, Ewa knew Lachlan was a damn sight more successful than he pretended. She also appreciated and respected his wish to remain anonymous.

"I might try that. After all, we're in the middle of nowhere." He studied her. "Why do you want tae be my model? I dinnae think…"

"I was an exotic dancer when my husband first saw me." She lowered her voice. "My body has been the custody of others for longer than I care to remember. I am finally reclaiming it."

"If you put it like that, I cannae say no."

"What is the procedure? Do I have to stand still for hours?"

"Nah. I'd take some photographs and work fae those."

"Get your camera, then." She downed her glass of wine and poured another.

"You eastern Europeans, eh?" Lachlan pointed to his phone. "The quality on that is perfectly fine."

"I am ready." Ewa got up and pulled her top over her head.

"Woah!" Lachlan's eyes widened. "Steady on."

"I do not want a sculpture of my t-shirt and jeans. There is no need to avert your eyes. I am not shy."

"Obviously."

"Then I do not see a problem." She unfastened her bra and let it fall. Lachlan's throat constricted.

"I might need some more wine, too." He took a gulp as Ewa kicked off her shoes and struggled out of her jeans.

"You can keep the panties on." Lachlan rasped. "I can…"

"Don't be silly." She peeled the satin triangle off, twirled it around one finger and launched it at him. "You gave me the freedom to act however I please. I would be foolish not to take advantage of that."

"It's not *you* taking advantage I'm worried about." Lachlan peeled the underwear off his head.

"Are you saying you find me attractive?"

"I'm not a bloody monk."

"You are also free, yet you do not seem to cherish the fact."

Ewa lay down on the couch and rested her head on one hand.

"It is like the movie Titanic, yes? That is my favourite film."

"And I'm getting a sinking feeling."

"This is not the reaction I was hoping for," Ewa laughed. "But if you wish to keep things… professional, I am used to that."

"Again, not what I meant."

"Then do your artistic work." She turned her face to the left. "This is my best side, though it is my figure I want you to concentrate on."

"That's not going tae be a problem." Lachlan moved around her, taking pictures from all angles. His hands were shaking.

"I know you are not gay, my friend. I have asked around." Ewa shifted slightly to get more comfortable. "And you are attractive. Why do you have no woman in your life?"

"I like my own company?" Lachlan trotted out his familiar line.

"Not true. You always seem very happy when I come over." She smiled impishly. "I also enjoy coming over. And over."

"You're doing this on purpose." Lachlan's voice was hoarse. "But I'm just going tae take pictures, nothing more. You're a vulnerable…"

"Scared is not the same as vulnerable." Ewa stretched. "And I am no longer scared. I have tried several times to, as the Scots say, to chat you up. You are resistant to my charms."

"You have the most perfect body I ever set eyes on," Lachlan said. "But I am *not* going to take advantage of your gratitude."

"I am grateful, yes." Ewa's eyes clouded. "But do not presume to guess my motivation in some outdated, manly fashion. I like you, but I am far from a swooning damsel. For years I used this body as a tool."

She indicated herself.

"To gain my objectives. To entice. To survive. All it achieved was to move me out of one bad situation and into another."

She smiled sadly.

"I never got to use it for my own pleasure, with someone I care about and trust. This is something I would like to do."

Lachlan reddened.

"Perhaps I do not know how to show my affection any other way. Does it matter?"

"It matters to me."

"Oh well." She slid a slim hand between her legs. "If you wish to be an observer, so be it. I would rather you were watching than doing this on my own and imagining you with me."

Her fingers moved faster and her eyelids fluttered. Lachlan watched, transfixed, as she softly moaned.

"Wait." He grabbed her wrist.

"You want me to stop?"

"No." His resolve finally broke. "But you'll need both hands to undress me."

He slid his fingers inside her and she gasped.

Lachlan sank down and crushed his lips against hers.

"I've come over all hot and bothered," Dark gasped. "And a bit jealous, to be honest."

"She was an amazing woman," Lachlan admitted. "But so are you."

"Why did she leave, Lachlan?"

"Dark," he sighed. "There's something I have to tell you about myself. It's not very nice and the reason I dinnae mix with people."

"Not yet." She put a finger to his lips. "In a couple of days, you can reveal all your secrets, if you still want that. But not until I can reciprocate."

"Could you *be* any more opaque?"

"Please have confidence in me," she begged. "You don't have the answers I'm looking for but I know who does. Once I've spoken to him, we can both open up properly and let the chips fall where they may."

"God, you're exciting when you talk like that. I'm in."

"Good. Now, fuck me again. I'm competitive too."

Dark's Cottage 2024

Dark and Lewis

In the morning, they paid their bill and checked out.

"I'll drive you to your cottage." Lachlan tapped his nose. "Just in case someone is hanging around with an anti-tank gun."

"My friend Lewis will be there by now," Dark said. "I have to talk to him. He can escort me over to yours afterwards."

"I'm not letting you out of my sight until this is over," Lachlan objected.

"You gave me a pretty speech about women being the equal of men," Dark reminded him. "So, let's not get all 19th century about things. Lewis is no wimp, I assure you."

"Fuck. Hoisted on my own petard."

"I don't have a clue what that meant but stick to your word."

"Hurry back." Lachlan pulled her into an embrace. "I couldn't bear it if I found you face down in a pond riddled with bullets."

"Say, *what* now?"

"I got a weird sense of humour." Then his mouth set in a grim line. "But I'm serious. I'm a pacifist but tell this Lewis, if he lets anything happen tae you, he'll regret being born."

Dark searched his face for any trace of humour.

There was none.

Dark arrived at the cottage to find Lewis's car parked outside. When she came through the front door, he was sitting on the couch eating a tube of Pringle crisps.

"Hi, Billy," she said nonchalantly.

"Long time no see, Dark." He jumped up and hugged her. Suddenly, he stiffened and pulled away.

"Wait... *What* did you just call me?"

"Billy Milne." Dark pushed him onto the couch. "Don't even try to deny it."

"I won't," he said quietly. "How long have you known?"

"Quite a while. I just wasn't sure how best to use the information."

"I never wanted to lie to you in the first place. You're like my wee sister."

"You did anyway." She sat next to him. "You lied about your name. About how long you've known Spiral. About who he was. Everything."

Billy tried to look away, but she grabbed his chin.

"When I told you I was in Aftonhouse, you must have known I'd meet Lachlan Robertson." She fixed him with an intense stare. "Why didn't you tell me he was Spiral Wood?"

"Because he isn't," Billy replied sorrowfully. "Spiral is *not* Lachlan Robertson. He didn't recognise you, did he?"

"No. And he still doesn't know who I really am." Dark went to the memento box and opened it. "I recovered a few printouts from Spiral's shredder, by the way. Things about a final con he obviously never meant me to see."

"Oh shit."

"We've both got surprises to drop, I suppose."

"I thought *this* was part of Spiral's last con when I first found it." She took a carefully assembled A4 sheet from the box and handed it over. "But when he opened the door to me and introduced himself as Lachlan Robertson, there was absolutely no recognition in his eyes. Even a master like Spiral couldn't fake that kind of reaction.

Billy glanced at the contents. It was a magazine clipping from *The Medical News.*

Dissociative Identity Disorder (DID) is a mental disorder where a person has two or more distinct personalities. The thoughts, actions, and behaviours of each personality may be completely different.

Trauma often causes this condition, particularly during childhood. These fragmented personalities, or alters, can take control of the person's identity for some time. The primary identity is generally more passive and usually unaware of a secondary character.

Split personalities often have their own distinct name, moods and vocabulary. But they are normally temporary and will fade away.

"I pretended not to recognise him either. Figured, if I played along, it might give me time to work out what exactly the fuck was going on."

"I don't need to read this," Billy handed the sheet back. "I've always known about Lachlan's condition."

"Yet, you never thought to fill me in?"

"Spiral pleaded with me not to," he said defensively. "Lachlan doesn't even know his alter ego exists."

He twiddled his thumbs nervously."

"But I don't understand why *you* didn't tell Lachie everything. He'd have no choice but to accept it. I'm sure the year-long gap in his memory is causing him no end of puzzlement and distress."

"Don't lay all this on me," Dark snapped. "I can't believe you never told Lachlan about Spiral. You were his best friend."

"He's home where he belongs and, hopefully, happy to be there. He doesn't need to know the things that Spiral might have done in his name. Especially not if it sends him to prison."

"Yeah, we'll get to that." Dark looked at the article. "It says here the new personality can be triggered by childhood trauma."

"And Lachlan's sure as hell had one of those."

"That's putting it mildly."

"Lachie could never have left his mum and brother in that snowstorm, so someone else took over and made the hard decision."

"Spiral Wood."

"He didn't have a name, to begin with," Billy said. "In public, Frankie Cameron and I still called him Lachie. But he wasn't Lachlan anymore. So, in private, we named him after the place where he lived. Spiral Wood."

"That's what Frankie didn't want to tell me."

"She's fiercely protective of him. Both of them, in fact."

"So are you, obviously."

"Spiral did the things my dad wanted me to do until the Laird thought I wasn't fit to take over his operation," Billy replied dolefully. "I reckon that was his plan to keep me from turning into my father."

"Highly ironic."

"It hurt, but what could I do? He would have stuck with me if the positions had been reversed."

"And he changed back when his own dad died?"

"That drug-addled shit? Before we knew what had happened, Spiral was Lachie again. Lachlan couldn't remember a damned thing about leaving his mother and brother - or the months afterwards. Can you imagine what that did to him? He thought he was a craven coward and had blanked the incident out."

He shook his head.

"The saddest part is, Spiral did exactly the right thing. It was a slim chance and it didn't work. But it was their *only* chance."

"Christ. So, all Lachlan remembers is the fact that he deserted them?"

"That and the fact that he seemed to have become Big Don's unofficial second in command. Me and Frankie convinced him he'd had a nervous breakdown. Seemed like the kindest thing to do."

He patted his knees, ill at ease.

"I've been waiting for an angry phone call ever since you got here." His eyes narrowed. "*Why* didn't you tell Lachie the truth, Dark? Please tell me you're not pulling a con of your own."

"I suppose I am."

"The poor guy's been through enough," Billy protested. "Look, if it's cash you want, I'll split everything I have with you."

"I'm not interested in money."

"Then what?"

"I need to talk to Spiral."

"He's gone," Billy sighed. "Let it alone."

"And I'm trying to bring him back. *That's* why I haven't told Lachlan the truth."

"What have you done, Dark?"

"According to this article, trauma can bring out the, what's it called?" She scanned the page. "The alter."

"What have you done?" Billy repeated.

"I pretended there was a prowler outside his balcony. I held a knife to his throat. Even shot up his house."

"You have a *gun?*"

"Spiral left one in his memento box."

"For fuck's sake!"

"Nothing worked, Bill."

"That's cause Spiral doesn't appear to *protect* Lachie or the people he loves," Billy groaned. "Lachlan can do that perfectly well on his own and he sure as hell doesn't scare easily. But he's also the nicest and most decent guy you could meet."

He tapped the magazine clipping.

"Lachie would have died before he left his mother and brother, no matter how sensible an option it was. Only Spiral could make the hard choice."

"I finally realise that," Dark replied wistfully. "Spiral Wood carries out any unthinkable task Lachie would never be able to stomach."

"Exactly." Billy picked at his lip.

"Couldn't he get professional help?"

"They made him talk to some local council shrink after his mum died - but she never cottoned on that she was dealing with Spiral. He just claimed he'd blanked out the trauma and couldn't remember anything."

"A con man right from the get-go, eh?" Dark mused. "That ruse came in pretty handy for him later."

"What do you mean?"

"Forget it."

"I talked Lachie out of getting any more therapy, so he chose solitude. After 20 years and no sign of Spiral, I was sure it was a one-off."

Dark thought about Gordon Crabbe. He'd met Spiral Wood, without a doubt. She wondered how many others had, without realising it. Still, no point in bringing that up now.

"So, what brought him back this time?"

"Eva. Eva Stone." His voice dipped. "Lachie doesn't know what happened to her and I don't want to tell him."

"Then tell me," Dark whispered. "Please."

Billy took a deep breath.

"Just over a year ago, I did a solo job for my father. That was unusual in itself and I got the strangest vibe about it. So, I asked Lachie to come along for backup."

He closed his eyes.

"It went horribly wrong…"

-Part V-

At the lonely crossroads
Where there was once a gallows
He forgets the wind for a moment

His watch is at his ear
The sky threatens a storm
He wishes he could take all four roads
He takes all four roads

Tony   Conner.   *The   Memoirs   of   Uncle   Harry*

Merchiston Point 2023

Lachlan, Billy and Ewa

Billy reached the truck. One of the skinheads was pulling an unconscious woman from the interior, hands tied behind her back. Billy could smell a lingering trace of chloroform.

"What the fuck is going on?" he demanded.

"You were told not to return until we were gone," the villain said. "This is why I hate dealing with amateurs."

"Jesus," Billy gasped. "That's Eva Stone. We're neighbours!"

"This is Mrs. Martin Cindrić," The scarred brute grunted. "It has taken her husband a great deal of time and money, trawling the underbelly of Europe, to finally find someone who knew where she was."

The hoodlum was obviously referring to Billy's father.

"So, this wanker is kidnapping his own wife and my dad helped?" Indignation overcame Billy's shame and fear. "What kind of evil fucktard are you working for?"

"She is his property."

"No. She's one of us now, pal."

"This is the agreed transaction with Don Milne. Her life in exchange for yours." The man reached into his waistband and drew a gun. "Since you are here, you will carry her to the dingy."

The other bruiser took out a satellite phone.

"I shall call Mr. Cindrić and ask whether we take you with us to explain yourself or shoot you on the spot." He gave a cruel leer. "If you are lucky, he will order you executed."

"Let's not be hasty." Billy put his hands up. "I can still go back the way I came. No harm done."

"It is too late. You do not ever disobey Mr. Cindrić."

"Don't you know who my dad is?" Billy stammered.

"He is a big fish in a tiny pond. My employer is a shark who rules the…"

There was a crack from the distance and one of the skinheads slammed against the side of the vehicle, a red patch blossoming on his chest.

His cohort jerked around, pistol raised. There was another pop and he shot backwards as if an invisible hand had tossed him carelessly away.

Billy put a hand over his mouth, trying not to retch. There was a neat hole in the man's forehead.

Lachlan came walking down the track, the barrel of his rifle smoking.

"You killed them!" Billy's head was spinning. "I thought you said the gun wasn't loaded?"

"I found ammunition in my pocket."

Lachlan raised the weapon and pointed it at Billy.

"I'm pretty certain they had no intention of letting either of you go. Now untie Ewa, then convince me you had nothing to do with her abduction."

"We've been friends since we were kids." Billy didn't try to beg or run. "I would never knowingly be part of something like this, Lachie."

"I'm not Lachlan, Bill."

"Say *what* now?"

"Don't you remember me?"

The voice was different. So was the posture. Billy recalled both from when he was a teenager. He took a shuddering intake of breath.

"*Spiral?*"

"The one and only. It's been a while."

"Many years, buddy."

"If you had known what was going on, I suppose you wouldn't have brought Lachlan along." Spiral lowered his gun, face expressionless. "Ewa and Lachlan were an item, by the way. They just didn't tell anyone."

Billy went white.

"You may as well shoot me now," he said. "I fucking mean it. I don't know how I'll live with what I've done."

"It wasn't you. It was Big Don." Spiral sighed. "In fairness, he was obviously trying to save you."

"That's no excuse."

"I know. We're going put these bastards in the dingy, take them out to that launch and scupper it. Then we'll go home." Spiral began to untie Ewa. "It looks like she's been drugged."

"My father may have been coerced into this." Billy hung his head. "But I can't forgive him. I'm done with the man."

"Good." Spiral gently lifted the woman and put her in the cab. "As for Martin Cindrić? He's going to regret the day he pulled this little stunt."

Daylight was fading by the time they reached Aftonhouse. Spiral detoured and stopped near the Laird's mansion.

"Can you get inside without anyone seeing you?"

"Dad will be out somewhere crowded, so he has an alibi," Billy said. "Probably in Oban. He'll have left a couple of his heavies but they'll be at their bothies by now. I have keys and codes for the alarms."

"And his safe?"

"He treated me like I was invisible most of the time. But I've got eyes. I saw him open it often enough to know the combination."

"Take everything. The money. The ledgers. Everything."

"I'll be back in fifteen minutes."

Billy was true to his word. Then they drove to Lachlan's house.

"Fetch a shovel from the shed outside, put it in the back of the truck and hide the vehicle in the wood," Spiral commanded. "We'll go to Ewa's cottage in my car and make it look like she went on a trip. Sow as much confusion as we can."

Spiral went inside and packed a suitcase. When they arrived at Ewa's house, she was finally beginning to stir. Spiral jumped into the back and put his arms round her.

Her eyelids fluttered open, a silent scream forming on her lips.

"It's all right. It's OK." Spiral rocked her. "I've got you. You're safe."

"Lachie?" she pulled him tight. "Thank God you are here."

"I won't let anyone hurt you."

"My husband," she stammered. "I never dreamed he would find me."

She looked around in panic.

"Am I home? How did you rescue me?"

"This is going to take some explaining," Billy mumbled. "On everyone's part."

"Later. First, we're going to whisk you away and give you another new identity." Spiral finally released her. "Don't worry. Me and Bill will come with you."

"My husband will hunt me down eventually, no matter where I go. I realise that now."

"You have my solemn word it will never happen," Spiral promised. "But get out for a moment. I need to take a selfie of us together."

"Are you fucking serious?" Ewa pouted. "I was just kidnapped."

"It's important."

"All right. You did just save me."

"Say cheese!" He put his head on her shoulder and held up his phone. "Pretend to be blissfully happy."

"I have plenty of experience doing that." Ewa faked a delighted smile, while Spiral snapped a few pictures.

"Right. Let's get the hell out of dodge. On the way, Billy and I have quite the story to tell you."

He indicated his car.

"We'll start off in this, though we can steal another later. Working for Big Don taught us a certain set of… useful skills."

"He means unlawful," Billy grunted. "Where exactly are we heading?"

"You always wanted to go to Edinburgh, so that'll do for now." Spiral opened the door and indicated for Ewa to climb back in. "You're going to use the Laird's underground contacts to get us all new identities. Don's money will ensure their silence."

"I can manage that," Billy sniffed. "What should I call myself?"

"World's your oyster, buddy. Pick something exotic."

"Lewis. After Lewis Gilbert, the silent film star."

"Whatever floats your boat, Lew."

"I like it." He struck a heroic pose. "After this, however, I'm staying firmly on the right side of the law."

"I agree with the first part." Spiral waited until Ewa was in the car, then closed the door so she couldn't hear. "But we need to continue being bad guys, to some extent. Mix with the dark side."

"Why?"

"Because I want to discover exactly who Martin Cindrić is. Then figure out the best way I can get to him."

"Lachlan isn't going to be back for a while," Billy whispered. "Is he?"

"Lachlan Robertson is tough. He's also a gentle soul who wouldn't harm a fly, no matter how provoked. He certainly can't take on a bastard like Ewa's husband."

Spiral gave a wolfish grin.

"That's my job."

Dark's Cottage 2024

Dark and Billy

By the time Billy finished his story, Dark was in tears.

"Is Ewa all right?" she asked.

"Yeah. She tried to make it work with Spiral but it only lasted a few days. It was Lachlan she adored. Spiral was too different." Billy smiled wryly. "Nor was he particularly enamoured with her. See, he understood something that Lachlan refused to accept."

"What was that?"

"Ewa cared deeply about Lachie but it was passion, not love. What's more, Lachie didn't love Ewa. He just felt obligated to return her affections and, being a decent guy, convinced himself it was something more. Spiral had no such scruples. He had a lust for life… and for other women. Until he met you."

Bill ran a hand through his thick hair.

"He gave Eva some money and she moved to London. The bigger the population, the longer it would take her husband to find her. In… theory."

"So… what *was* Spiral's last con?" Dark asked. "It sounded like he intended to betray her for money but that can't be it."

"Not at all! His concern was always keeping Eva safe. It's what Lachlan would have wanted. But only Spiral could do what was needed to make it a certainty." He pursed his lips. "I don't know exactly what transpired after Spiral returned to Aftonhouse but I can make a fair guess."

"I think I can too."

"Lachie may not have a clue about Spiral Wood but Spiral has all of Lachlan Roberson's memories." Billy pointed an imaginary weapon at her. "And his skills."

"Including being an expert shot?"

"Including being an expert shot."

Merchiston Point 2024

Spiral and Martin Cindrić

---

olding a waterproof briefcase, Martin Cindrić stepped out of his motor launch and onto the shingle. The dawn mist was only just beginning to clear.

He scanned the surrounding hills. Four snipers were hidden there and had been lying in wait since last night, wrapped in camouflaged sleeping bags. Cindrić wasn't the type to take chances.

His plan was simple. Show the informant his money and get Ewa's location. Have his people check it out. If the mystery man was bullshitting, he would die a painful death. If he was telling the truth, the result would be the same. And Martin would have his wife back.

Martin Cindrić smiled to himself. He was a wary man. His profession necessitated that. Yet, the naked picture of his wife had incensed him, causing Cindrić to throw caution to the wind. He had given a lot of thought about the terrible things he would do to Ewa. He was going to enjoy all of it.

He got out a satellite phone and held it to his ear.

"Are you in place?"

We have men stationed across Dundee, came the reply. *Whatever location we are given, we can be at it in ten minutes.*

"Excellent. Wait for my instructions."

What if she is not there?

"It's six in the morning and my wife was always a late sleeper. If there is nobody at home, I will assume our informant is lying and he will suffer accordingly."

He was going to suffer, regardless. Cindrić sat down on a rock and removed his gloves. He had little doubt who the snitch was. That little shit, Billy Milne, who had double-crossed him last time and killed his men. Cindrić had spent valuable time and resources looking for him, to no avail.

Big Don Milne had fought back rather than betray any clue as to the whereabouts of his son - and died in the attempt. Stupid fool. The boy had no such sense of honour.

His men made it look like a suicide but that avenue for information had been lost. The only other person in Aftonhouse Billy Milne seemed close to was a man called Lachlan Robertson. He had also vanished before Cindrić could question him.

No matter. Now Milne had gotten greedy and that would be his downfall.

Cindrić shivered with anticipation, unfastening his coat and shifting the shoulder holster to a more comfortable position. The snipers were only a backup. He intended to force Billy onto the launch and back to the yacht, where his remaining two crewmen were waiting.

After that, he would have time to make him properly sorry.

There was a faint crack in the distance and what felt like a punch in his gut. Cindrić looked down in surprise.

A pool of red was spreading from a hole in his jersey. He slid off the rock, crying in pain and scurried behind it for shelter. But it was too small for him to hide properly.

"Help!" he shouted. "Get me to the boat. Now!"

The snipers hesitated. They had no idea where the shot came from and revealing their positions would leave them exposed.

"Come down here and take me to the boat!" Cindrić screamed. "Or you and your families are dead."

The sharpshooters emerged from their hiding places and scurried down the slopes towards him.

"Shield me," he groaned, indicating vaguely. "The shot came from somewhere up there."

Shouldering their rifles, each man took an arm and leg and shuffled him towards the water, forming a human wall between their boss and his assailant.

"I do not understand," Cindrić rasped through gritted, bloody teeth. "I have the money."

One of the men stumbled and fell. There was another retort and a hole blossomed in Cindrić's forehead. His body went limp.

The men dropped his corpse and unslung their weapons.

"I have no beef with you," Spiral Wood yelled from his hiding place. "But don't doubt I'll drop you all before you can reach proper cover."

Cedric's men looked around. On the flat ground, there were virtually no places to conceal themselves.

"Take the money and divide it up with the crew if you wish," Spiral yelled. "Say I came with an army, and you put up a hell of a fight. Say you were outnumbered and I took the cash."

The men hesitated.

"Your boss is dead. You may as well get something out of it before some other fucker takes his place."

There was a muttered discussion among the thugs. They looked up and nodded assent.

"Just know, if you ever come back," Spiral continued. "I'll kill every one of you."

"We have no reason to return," one shouted. "Cindrić has no heirs to avenge him and the woman was *his* foolish obsession, not ours. This is over."

"I know," Spiral yelled back. "That's why I'm letting you leave alive."

The men carried Cindrić's body to the dinghy, dumped it unceremoniously into the stern and headed out to sea.

Spiral stood up, shaking from the spike of adrenaline. It was over. He pulled out his burner phone and dialled Dark's number. But the location was too isolated and there was no reception.

It didn't matter. He would be back in Edinburgh in a few hours. With their leader dead, Cindrić's minions would leave Dundee, unaware they had been in the wrong town the whole time and with no incentive to ever return. Billy and Ewa were finally safe.

It was a mile to the field where he had parked his stolen car, hidden in a small copse of trees off the main road.

Spiral walked with a spring in his step. He felt no guilt over killing Cindrić. The man deserved everything he got. His only emotion was one of elation. Soon, he could be with Dark again. She would have questions, of course. Questions he did not want to answer. But he owed Dark the truth, and he would finally tell her.

He looked around at the sun shining on the hills. God, this place was beautiful.

Dark would forgive him; he was convinced of it. It might take a while but he would be persistent. When she eventually relented, he intended to ask for her hand in marriage. He grinned to himself. What an old-fashioned phrase to describe the future.

He fished in his pocket, unwrapped a sandwich and bit into it.

They would have kids. A boy and a girl, maybe. He'd never stray. He loved her too much. They'd live a normal life. Settle in suburbia. He'd have a garage where he could write at night. He'd finally let her see his deepest thoughts and she would be impressed by his imagination. He would be a whole person.

He let his mind drift as he walked, soaking up the gorgeous surroundings.

Things were going to be all right.

By the time Spiral reached the main road, he had forgotten the stolen car existed. He stood by the grass verge, lost and disoriented. He had been with Billy Milne in a van, doing some job but the details were fuzzy. He looked around in confusion. It was the same place, he was sure of that. However, there was no sign of Billy or the vehicle.

What the fuck was going on?

A car drew up beside him and the window slid down.

"Why are you in the middle of nowhere, Lachie?" Elspeth leaned out. "Where's your car? We're quite aways from your house."

"I… I don't know."

"You don't *know*?"

"I must have hit my head or something."

"Hop in and I'll give you a lift back. Then you should call a doctor."

"Is that all right?"

"I was going shopping in Oban but I don't mind detouring. Can't just leave you standing here."

"Thank you." Lachlan climbed in, not sure of what else to say. What *was* he doing in the middle of nowhere?

"Welcome back from Europe, by the way. I presume that's where you've been."

"Eh… I have."

Elspeth glanced at the rifle.

"Hey. I thought you didn't hunt?"

"Ummm. I'm using it as a walking stick?"

"Don't be picking up those weird foreign ways," Elspeth laughed. "Where were you this time? Italy? France? It's been a pretty long trip."

"How long since you've seen me, exactly?"

"More than a year."

"Aye. I was… eh… touring around. Listen, I need to talk to Bill. Have you seen him?"

"What? He left Aftonhouse at the same time as you." His smile became strained. "I hoped perhaps that *you'd* know his whereabouts."

"I didn't even realise he was gone."

"Seriously? You and Bill were never big on using social media but didn't you keep in touch with anyone?"

"Not really." Lachlan's mouth was so dry he could hardly talk. "What about Big Don?"

"I'm so sorry, Lachie." Elspeth put a hand on his arm. "The Laird died months ago."

Lachlan turned and stared morosely out of the window. A year. Where had he been for a year?

What had he *done*?

"Oh Christ," he muttered to himself. "It's happened again."

When Elspeth dropped him off, he ran to Ewa's house. Perhaps she could shed some light on what had occurred.

It was completely deserted.

Dark's Cottage 2024

Dark and Billy

"Spiral desperately wanted to come back to you," Billy said. "He was also fully aware he'd been brought into existence to get rid of the threat to Lachlan, Ewa and myself. Once he'd achieved that, his raison d'être would be gone."

"If he really loved me, it should have been enough to keep him around!"

"That's what he told me, at great length, many times." Billy bit his lip. "As if repeating the words often enough would make them true. I think he tried to fool himself into believing things would work out."

"Why didn't they?"

"You can't con a con man. I presume, deep down, he felt you deserved better than a shadow."

"Spiral wasn't a shadow! He was real to *me*. I was crazy about him."

"Believe it or not, I loved Spiral as much as I love Lachie," Billy retorted. "But he never stood a chance of hanging on and I'm afraid I'm OK with it."

"That's why you warned me off." Dark smiled wanly. "Thank you, even if I didn't pay the slightest attention."

"You're pig-headed. Like him."

"I saw a different side to Spiral, Bill. He was wonderful in his own warped way. I would never have believed he was capable of killing."

"Given the right circumstances, he was capable of *anything*."

"The strange thing is, I would have forgiven what he did to Martin Cindrić." Dark shook her head. "The bastard deserved it."

"I was fine with that too. I guess, when push comes to shove, none of us are as decent as we like to make out."

"Lachlan is."

"Without doubt." Billy stuffed a handful of crisps into his mouth. "Are you ready to come back to Edinburgh? I'll see you're OK."

"There's a slight complication," Dark said. "I'm staying. See, I've fallen for Lachlan."

"I can't even begin to start processing that." To her amazement, Billy grinned. "But you were good for Spiral, so why not? All you have is spend a lifetime hiding the fact that you were also in love with his evil twin."

"When you put it like that, it sounds pretty romantic."

"It's going to be a damned big barrier to happiness, kid. Lachlan would be devastated to know what his substitute personality did. And forget about a social life. He was a hermit before. He'll be ten times worse now, I imagine."

"I wouldn't bet on it. As soon as I turned up, he invited me in. Then he agreed to go to dinner. *Then* he showed me his etchings."

"Clever Lachie. He was trying to find answers without giving too much away." Billy laughed softly. "In case he'd done something terrible and you were an undercover detective or something."

"Or something," Dark agreed. "Point is, he enjoyed it. And he's after the truth, Bill."

"Then break it to him gently. Please."

"Not an option."

"Why not?"

"I told you." Dark shook her head. "I *have* to talk to Spiral one last time. Even if it's only for a few minutes."

"Lachlan isn't afraid of anything, except himself. You already know you can't bring Spiral back by threats or violence."

"I get that now. Spiral only appears when Lachlan has to make a choice too terrible to contemplate."

"I don't like where this conversation is heading."

"This is my last con, mate." Dark patted her companion's shoulder. "You're going to help me, though I warn you, it'll be dangerous."

"For me?"

"Definitely."

"Will Lachie get hurt?"

"No."

"Shit. Go on then."

Dark told him her plan. Billy waited until she was finished.

"Dangerous? That's suicidal. You're placing a lot of faith in love."

"What else is there to have faith in?"

"Point taken." He placed the empty Pringles tube on the table and clapped his hands anxiously.

"Besides, I owe you. Spiral, too, for that matter."

As they drove to Lachlan's house, Billy stared out of the window at the green fields and high peaks gliding past.

"It's lovely here, isn't it?" he said. "I miss it."

"Do you miss Elspeth?"

"Fuck, yeah. I went out with a bunch of girls in Edinburgh but none of them compared." He waved a desultory hand in the air. "I well and truly burned that bridge, though. What the hell would I say to her?"

"I'm willing to forgive Spiral for being a killer, you dick." Dark snorted. "Tell the truth. You were protecting her from Martin Cindrić. She's still holding a torch for you, by the way."

"She is?" Billy looked astonished.

"Come back," Dark cajoled. "You can't stay in Edinburgh cheating people forever. You'll end up in jail."

"I stopped all that when you and Spiral did," Billy replied. "I'm currently considering my limited career options."

"Sorry for your loss, by the way. With your dad and everything."

"Thank you but we weren't close."

"I presume Big Don's mansion belongs to you now."

"It does."

"And his legal fortune."

"I have a nest egg the size of an ostrich. Not an ostrich egg. A whole ostrich." He screwed up his face. "I could sell it but Elspeth would never leave Frankie or the shop, so what would *I* do? Rattle around in that huge place admiring the view? Play bingo at the village hall every Thursday?"

He traced a thick finger down the window.

"Aftonhouse is breathtaking. It's also off the beaten track and dying. Nobody ever comes here."

"They would if they had a good reason." A slow grin spread across Dark's face. "Your house has haulage sheds, doesn't it? And nice grounds."

"What do you propose? I build a winter wonderland and play Santa?" Billy patted his stomach. "I've put on weight but not that much."

"What about a world-class art gallery?"

"You angling to have your mum's circular saw blades on display?" he chuckled. "Spiral had a collection of fake Guarnerius Del Gesu violins I could borr…"

His voice trailed away.

"What exactly *are* you suggesting?"

"I'm suggesting using your property to exhibit pieces by a famous sculptor, who also happens to be your best pal." Dark's smile widened. "That would put Aftonhouse on the map for sure."

"Holy hell!"

"I could write a fine magazine piece about it. Oh. I already did. Just need to add in the Milne Gallery."

"You're a fucking genius!" Billy leaned over and kissed her cheek. "You think Lachie would go for it? He always wanted to stay anonymous."

"He isolates himself because he has missing blanks in his past. Once we fill those in, he won't have to."

"I never thought of it like that," Billy admitted. "I've been pretty dumb."

"I also know he's sick of being lonely. I'm sure he'd do anything for his oldest mate, especially if it meant you moved back."

"We should do it. Let's do it."

Billy nodded happily, already planning renovations in his head. As they drew close to their destination, he looked up.

"Don't get me killed, Dark," he warned. "Not now, I've got something to look forward to."

"I won't. You up for this?"

"Like you, I've always had a flair for the dramatic."

He opened the glove compartment and took out Spiral's gun.

They drew up outside Lachlan's house. Billy forced the woman from the car, weapon held against her head.

"Show yourself, Lachie!" he shouted. "I know you're there."

The front door opened and Lachlan stepped into the path, grasping his rifle.

"*Billy*," he gasped. "What the fuck are you doing?"

"I want my money," the man yelled back. "Or I screw up this bitch."

"I dinnae ken what you're talking about!" Lachlan's eyes widened. "Where have you been? Is it *you* who's been stalking me and shooting up my house?"

"Of course. You and this con woman swindled me out of everything I own. Come to get it back, buddy."

"I… I…"

"Don't plead innocence. I'm up to my neck in gambling debts and I'm desperate."

"I dinnae remember the last year," Lachlan pleaded. "I told everyone I'd been in Europe but I honestly don't know where I was or what I've done."

"Pull the other one, you wanker."

"If I did something tae hurt you, I'm sorry and we'll work it out. But I genuinely dinnae ken what's going on. You have tae believe me."

"I'm going to count to three." Billy lowered the barrel and pressed it against Dark's leg. "Then I kneecap her."

"No! I would never cheat you, Bill!"

"Don't let him hurt me!" Dark sobbed. "Give him what he wants."

"But I dinnae…"

"One…" Billy cocked the pistol. "Two…"

Lachlan's stance changed. The rifle snapped up and he aimed down the sight.

"I *will* kill you if you harm her, Bill," he said coldly, all trace of his highland accent gone. "Put a bullet in your head before you have time to pull the trigger. Don't make me do that to my best friend."

"It's him, isn't it?" Dark cried.

"Well, hello Spiral." Billy dropped the weapon. "Never been so pleased to see you."

Dark ran forward and launched herself into the man's arms, smothering him with kisses.

"Hey, toots." Spiral held her tight. "You're a sight for sore eyes."

Robertson Farm 2024

Spiral Wood

Spiral and Dark sat on the bench outside Lachlan's house, holding hands. Billy had tactfully gone for a walk, his mind buzzing with dreams and plans.

"What the fuck is this nonsense?" Spiral felt his long hair and stubbled grey beard. "Has Lachlan never heard of hair dye?"

"I think it's distinguished."

"I look like a middle-aged hipster." He touched Dark's cheek as if he could hardly believe she was real. "You brought me back. That was very clever. And extremely dangerous."

"Only for Billy."

"You're incorrigible. No wonder I was so in love with you."

"Was?"

"I won't be able to stay, toots." Spiral looked disconsolate. "I desperately want to. I tried to. But I need a certain set of… conditions to exist."

"Billy says you became a con man so you could track down Martin Cindrić," Dark said. "I'm betting it was also because you like living on the edge."

"Until I fell for you," Spiral admitted. "Then I wanted a normal life. A home. A car. A decent job. Kids, even."

He twined his fingers through hers.

"But I can't have that. Only Lachlan can." He gave a dry laugh. "Lachlan. The real, improved Spiral Wood."

He patted his hair and beard.

"Apart from a serious lack of personal grooming."

Dark hated the way he referred to himself in the third person. It was as if he'd already gone.

"I liked the old you just fine," she stalled. "Do you know about myself and Lachlan?"

"Yes. When I'm awake, I have his memories." He gave a wry smile. "You're a good match."

"I'm staying in Aftonhouse. Got to quite like it here. And I want to be a writer."

"Suits you. Perhaps you'll tell my story someday." Spiral squeezed her hand. "It'll give me a sense of... permanence."

"I'll make damned sure you're not forgotten."

"You know, people say when you die, your scattered atoms become part of something bigger." Spiral struggled for the right words. "It's still shit, though. I want to exist. I want to be *me*."

He gave up and blew a raspberry.

"Why *did* you bring me back? It's obviously painful for both of us."

"Three reasons. One: I need to know who Spiral Wood, my first true love, actually is. Because he's more than just some... mental aberration."

"You described me as childish once," he replied. "That was closer than you know. I'm someone who never had time to become fully formed. I'm Mr. Hyde to Lachlan's Dr Jeckyl. Pinnochio wanting to be a real boy. Peter Pan's escaped shadow."

"Don't put yourself down. I can't stand it."

"I'm sorry, but I don't feel the way other people do. It's like I'm an observer and there's a wall between me and the rest of the world. When you came along, you somehow opened a door and walked straight in. But you can come and go as you please. I can never leave."

Dark wiped at her eyes, trying to keep her emotions under control.

"I have a passion for life, toots," he continued. "I *love* life. I cram in as much as I possibly can in the time I have. But I don't enjoy it. That make sense? The wall is always there."

He gave a heartfelt sigh.

"You deserve more than a ghost made flesh." He looked up at the sky. "It's a shame because I tried *so* hard."

"You loved me back, Spiral. Didn't you?"

"With all my heart. Even if my heart wasn't as big as other people's."

"It was fucking big enough for me." Dark rested her head on his shoulder. "I'm sorry."

"Not your fault." Spiral brushed away a strand of stray hair. "What were the other reasons?"

"Two? To say I love you and always will and to apologise for not trusting you and walking out."

"Kind of beat you to the punch there, so it's me who should say sorry. Number three?"

"I'm pregnant."

Spiral jerked back.

"You're *what?*"

"Before you make a sarcastic comment, it's yours, not Lachlan's." She grimaced. "Well, you're the same person, sort of. But… you know what I mean."

"Are you keeping it?"

"Of course." She slapped his arm. "It's part of you."

"Lachlan's in for an almighty shock, huh?" Spiral was grinning from ear to ear. "He'll make a great dad, though."

"So would you, despite your… flaws."

"Delicately put."

"If it's a girl, I'm calling it Ewa. If it's a boy, Spiral. Non-negotiable."

"He'll get some shit at school over that."

"If he's like his father, either of them, he'll deal with it just fine." She rested a hand on his arm. "I'll make sure he knows all about you when he's old enough to understand."

"Break him in gently. I take it you're happy?"

"I'm happy."

"That's what I needed to hear." He looked across the landscape. The hills were glowing in the sunlight and the smell of cut grass drifted up from the meadows. "You should hold me now. I'm ready to go."

"Absolute bollocks."

"Of course I'm not ready!" Spiral laughed. "I'm also shit ton better as a boyfriend than that windbag, Lachlan Robertson." His tone grew serious. "I'm scared, though."

A single tear ran down his cheek.

"I need the last thing I see to be your face."

"Oh, Spiral." Dark reached round and kissed him on the lips.

"Life is beautiful, isn't it?" he whispered. It sounded more like a question than a statement. Something he'd never really known the answer to.

"Shhhh. It's all right." She pulled him closer. "Remember the feeling of the sun on your face. A cool wind rustling leaves in the trees. The tang of wood smoke in the air. You won't be able to sleep for dreaming."

"I hope so. I love you, Dorothy."

Spiral shut his eyes and laid his head on her lap until he drifted away.

She was still stroking his hair when Billy approached.

"Is he?"

"Spiral's gone, Bill."

"Oh." Billy was crestfallen. "I wanted to say goodbye but didn't think I should interrupt."

"Shake him." Dark wiped her eyes and pulled herself together. "Say hello instead."

Billy gave the prone figure a gentle push. The man yawned and stretched. His eyes opened.

"I must hae fallen asleep," he said groggily.

"Hi, stranger."

"Billy?" Lachlan sat bolt upright. "What the hell are you doing here? Where have you *been*?"

He shook his head in confusion.

"Dark? What the fuck is going on?"

"We have a bit of a story to tell you," Dark said. "And it's a doozy, so I recommend you get yourself a stiff whisky."

Robertson Farm 2024

Lachlan

Lachlan sat in silence while they told him everything. He didn't interrupt except to ask for another whisky halfway through their tale.

When they were done, Dark and Billy waited.

"I killed people." His voice was expressionless.

"No. Spiral Wood did."

"This is what I was afraid of." He couldn't look them in the eye. "That I'd done something terrible during the last year."

"Spiral rescued Ewa," Dark said. "Stopped her husband from taking her back."

"What about my mum and my brother? He abandoned them. *I* abandoned them!"

"Neither of you did," Billy corrected. "Spiral went for the option that gave them the best chance, even if it failed. You would have stayed and died for nothing."

"I killed people," Lachlan repeated. "I need tae go to the police."

"Only if you want me and Dark to end up in the cell next to you, as accessories after the fact." Billy pointed out. "Ours won't even be padded."

"There's no proof you did anything to anyone," Dark interrupted. "But Bill and I would go down for conning people."

"Fuck." Lachlan ran a hand through his hair.

"You are *not* Spiral Wood." Dark took his hand. "Billy and I can vouch for that."

"You and Frankie should hae told me years ago." Lachlan glared balefully at his friend. "It wasnae fair to keep that from me."

"Really? Cause you're taking it *so* well."

Dark elbowed him in the ribs.

"Yes," Billy relented. "We should have."

"You too." He withdrew his hand from Dark's. "You used me."

"I did." The woman hung her head. "I came here to find Spiral and refused to let anything get in my way."

"What was she supposed to say, buddy?" Billy sprang to her defence. "Hi. I'm your girlfriend but you don't remember me. So, let's start again, eh? Oh, by the way, I'm pregnant."

"Excuse me?" Lachlan's eyes widened.

"I overheard Dark in passing."

"He doesn't know that part, you moron," Dark hissed. "I told Spiral in confidence!"

"He's just been insisting on the truth." Billy looked abashed. "I think we need to put all our cards on the table."

"Stop talking about me like I'm not here." Lachlan snapped. "And I dinnae want tae be a father. Especially with someone I hardly know."

"I can understand that." Dark got up. "I didn't mean for anything like this to happen and I apologise for the hurt I've caused."

Her face crumpled.

"You needn't worry. I'll head back to Edinburgh tomorrow and you won't have to see me again."

She elbowed her way out of the door.

"Forty years I've known you, Lachie," Billy snapped. "Never seen you be such an asshole before."

"What do you expect?" Lachlan retorted. "Put yourself in my shoes."

"It's a shock, I'll bet." Billy poured them both another shot. "The great Lachlan Robertson finally finding something he's afraid of."

"And what would that be?"

"Letting someone in."

"For Christ's sake, Bill. I care about Dark but I'd like to have done a bit of proper romancing before I decided to have a child with her."

"Put yourself in my shoes. That's what you said." Billy pointed to the open doorway. "Now, put yourself in that girl's shoes. In the space of one hour, she's lost the two people she loved and the father of her child. One *can't* help her raise it. Turns out the other won't."

"It's mair complicated than that." Lachlan paused. "Aw, shit. I've used that line before."

"There's no easy answer to this, Lachie. But if you won't give the kid a home, I will. Dark deserves that much."

"Don't you understand?" Lachlan's eyes were red-rimmed. "When we lie in bed and Dark stares into my eyes, will she wish *Spiral* was the one looking back?"

"Not if you play your cards right."

"Good one." Lachlan chuckled despite himself.

"We've all been dealt a bad hand, you most of all. But it's what we have to work with."

"Only, there's a stray joker in the pack," Lachlan sniffed. "Spiral was obviously the love of Dark's life. She *said* so. What if I'm just a guy who reminds her of him? The rebound, if you like."

"Quit the poker analogies. It's not me you should ask, pal."

"You're right." Lachlan stood up. "Stay here. Help yourself to whisky."

"With pleasure." Billy gave his friend a slap on the rump. "Have a bit of faith in yourself, eh? In *her*. Don't be too chicken to say it."

"Say what?"

"Thirty years we've been friends, bud," Billy admonished. "We both know."

Lachlan went outside. Dark was crouched on the bench crying.

"Can't even smoke anymore." She wiped her eyes. "Or have a joint."

"I have one question." He sat down next to her. "What would you do if Spiral could come back for good?"

"I'd send him away." The reply was instant.

"Why? Because he'd be a bad father?"

"That's two questions. Three, actually."

"Indulge me."

"I think he'd make a great father." She glared at him. "What would you do if Ewa came back?"

"Tell her I found someone else."

"I'd say the same to Spiral." She wiped her eyes. "You know, he summed you up in one sentence. Better than I ever could."

"The cowardly bastard who tried tae steal his girl?"

"The real, improved Spiral Wood."

"A backhanded compliment if I ever heard one."

"I know what he meant," Dark said solemnly. "See, Billy thinks Spiral existed to make the hard choices you couldn't. But that's not strictly true. He always took the easy way out."

"I'm not sure what you mean."

"You'd have chased off Cindrić's goons without killing anyone, then found another way to save Ewa. You'd have rescued me without shooting Billy." She reached out and stroked his cheek. "And you would have stayed and died with your mum and brother."

"I guess I should be grateful to Spiral for stopping that."

"Moment of truth." Dark turned and looked Lachlan in the eye. "Want to know why I was so crazy about Spiral Wood?"

"Painful as the answer may be, yes."

"Because he tried his damnedest to be like you."

"Oh." Lachlan blinked.

"Sometimes, when I'm drifting off to sleep, I imagine Spiral's last con was engineering a subtle way for me to find the real deal. And it worked." Dark turned away and stared at the landscape, her voice lowering to a whisper. "Because I love you."

Lachlan reached out and turned her head towards him.

"I love you too. I honestly do."

He kissed her tenderly on the lips. Then leaned back and put a hand on her stomach.

"I'll love both of you."

"About fucking time." Billy stood in the doorway, grinning from ear to ear. "I was dreading the thought of having a kid cramp my style."

He raised his glass to them.

"Especially when there's a certain young lady I hope will forgive me."

Milne Mansion 2025

Everyone

The opening of the Milne Gallery was a big event. Lachlan's announcement of who W.H. Art really was had become national news. On the strength of that, Billy was able to obtain more works by established and up-and-coming artists.

Dark watched the crowds filing into the renovated warehouses. She carried baby Spiral in the crook of one arm. Elspeth and Frankie strolled over, beaming.

"I've sold more products in the last few days than I did in the previous year," Frankie said. "Aftonhouse Hotel is full and the restaurant is thinking of including vegan options."

She held out her arms.

"Can I carry the wee man for a while?"

"Be my guest." Dark handed the child to her. Frankie walked off, cooing over the infant.

Elspeth threw her arms around Dark and squeezed her tight. "Thank you *so* much."

"Don't thank me," Dark pointed. "Thank Bill."

Billy wandered over, looking overjoyed.

"I'd say this was a roaring success." He nodded towards Lachlan, signing autographs on the lawn. "I've booked a table for all of us at the inn tonight. We're going to party like it's 1999."

He winked at Dark.

"You did good, kid."

"The work was all yours."

"Come on. I'll show you around." Billy kissed Elspeth, hooked his arm through hers and escorted her away.

"Hiya Dark."

She glanced around. A young girl was standing behind her and it took a few seconds to register who she was.

"*Nancy?*"

"I saw Spiral's picture in the *Edinburgh Evening News*. Told my parents I had a sudden interest in sculpture and persuaded them to take me here."

She frowned.

"Spiral didn't seem to recognise me. And why is he calling himself Lachlan?"

"Invite your parents to the hotel tonight as my guests. I'll give you the sanitised version." Dark hugged the girl. "Are you doing OK?"

"I am. Passed my exams with flying colours and got a boyfriend. Still too young to do that thing in the garden, though."

"No hurry, girl."

"I know." She stepped back. "I better go find the parentals. They're probably admiring the fire extinguisher and discussing what it means."

She smirked and ran off.

"Can this day get any weirder?" Dark looked around. A couple were walking towards her, hand in hand. "I guess it could."

The woman had short blonde hair and Dark immediately recognised her.

"Ewa, I presume."

"May I have a moment, kochanie?" Ewa asked her partner. "I must talk to this lady."

"Of course. I'll look at the exhibits."

Once he was gone, Ewa glanced shyly at Dark.

"Billy invited me," she said. "I hope that is all right."

"Absolutely."

"I said hello to Lachlan but it was awkward. Anyway, it was you I mainly came to see." She lowered her voice. "Is it true? Is he gone?"

For a moment, Dark thought she was talking about Spiral. Then she nodded.

"Martin Cindrić will never bother you again."

"I did not think this could ever happen." The woman clasped both hands together. "Lachlan is a wonderful man but if I am to say sorry for your loss, will you understand?"

"I will indeed."

"Spiral freed me," Ewa said. "In a way, he gave his life to do so. God be with him. And you."

She gave a grateful smile and almost skipped away.

Dark turned around. In the distance, she could just make out the treetops of Spiral Wood. She no longer found it creepy, just a sad and lonely place, misunderstood and filled with secrets.

Now it had one more.

Inside the thickest part, where nobody would ever find it, she had buried Spiral's memento box next to her father's ashes.

She fingered the locket around her neck.

"Watch over us," she whispered. "My black hart."

Then she went to join her husband.

End

ABOUT THE AUTHOR

Jan-Andrew Henderson (J.A. Henderson) is the author of 40 children's, teen, YA, adult and non-fiction books. Published in the UK, Europe, USA, Australia and Canada, he has been shortlisted for fifteen literary awards and is the winner of the Doncaster Book Prize, the Aurealis Award and the Royal Mail Award.

www.janandrewhenderson.com

We hope that you enjoyed this title and look forward to many more to come. Please, leave us a review! Reviews matter to all of our authors.

Take a look at some of our other award-winning series at https://threeravenspublishing.com/series-universes/

Visit us at https://www.threeravenspublishing.com and sign up for our newsletter for the latest and greatest news on upcoming titles and events.

Other series and titles you might enjoy.

JOINT TASK FORCE 13
HOLDING THE LINE
BETWEEN HEAVEN AND HELL
AVAILABLE ON
AMAZON

B.E.N.T.
BIOLOGIC   ENHANCED   NASCENT   TALENT

STARFLIGHT

IT CAME FROM THE
TRAILER PARK

You can also keep up to date with our latest release announcements on Scifi.radio and get some of the best fandom programing on the planet.

Scifi for your Wifi

And don't forget to check out our other Sponsors and Affiliates

A southern Appalachian jewel for craft beer lovers, Buck Bald Brewing offers something for everyone.

To discover more visit us at buckbaldbrewing.com

Revolution X is a testament to the power of collaboration, blending four unique styles into a cohesive, revolutionary sound. When these four individuals unite, the result is nothing short of musical Revolution!

Would you like to learn how to write and market your own titles? The following affiliates links might be helpful.

Don't forget to check out the latest edition of Car Warriors: Autoduel Chronicle fiction series.

Comprised of active or retired servicemen and civilian volunteers, Shepherd's Men enthusiastically raises awareness and funds for the SHARE Military Initiative (SHARE) at Shepherd Center in Atlanta, GA.

This nationally renowned program focuses on assessment and treatment for American military veterans who have sustained mild to moderate Traumatic Brain Injury (TBI) and Post-Traumatic Stress Disorder (PTSD) during post-9/11 service.

Find out more at: https://www.shepherdsmen.com/

www.ingramcontent.com/pod-product-compliance
Lightning Source LLC
Chambersburg PA
CBHW061340310726
48974CB00001B/129